The Legends of Regia
BURNING BRIDGES

A NOVEL

Tenaya Jayne

Cold Fire Publishing LLC

Other titles by Tenaya Jayne

Blue Aspen

Forbidden Forest

Forest Fire

Verdant

Dark Soul

ISBN-13: 978-0-9882757-7-5

Cover Art created by Erika Doucesse

Edited by Amanda Fiske & Valerie Hatfield

Proofread by Ally Robertson

COLD FIRE PUBLISHING, LLC

All Rights Reserved

For Lauren…for your sweetness and your spine.

Prologue

For thousands of years, the Storytellers came to Regia. An enigmatic people most Regians considered on the edge of Divinity. The Storytellers traveled not through portals from their homeland, but on channels made of golden light. They never explained why they came, and they never stayed long. They brought with them the ability to reach inside individuals, pull out the cords of their deepest longings, and give it to them, if only for a few moments.

Some called it hallucination, some called it magic, but no matter the name, it was always born of love. Storytellers never worked one on one, but with small groups. Sometimes the *story* began with song. A Storyteller's voice could hypnotize anyone with only a few notes. The experience was different for each person listening. The story spoken, became a visual tapestry, moving and caressing the senses of the listeners. The crowd not only saw but also felt the story as if it were their own memory, and in a way, it was. Each person gave something to the Storyteller, an intangible part of themselves, the Storyteller in turn wove it into the story they created.

Storytellers were heart-readers, and the cracks and aches deep inside a person were as plain to them as the color of the person's eyes. But a story from a Storyteller was not just a quick whisper of wish fulfillment. It moved into the heart and took root, and it brought healing to the listener's mind and spirit. They could quell anger between enemies, and make the timid brave. They brought clarity, and clarity gave birth to peace.

However, in Regia's modern times, the Storytellers became fewer and fewer. On the rare occasion one would come, they would be exhausted within days from the demand for their services and would quickly leave.

The laws of Illumistice, the Storyteller's world, gave their youth, on the point of maturity, an opportunity to travel the channels for a set period of time, to learn about themselves, and make the decision if they desired to live on another world, or embrace their destiny back home. There was only one stipulation in the law, besides the time limit; once you came home, you could never travel the channels again.

Journey was a healer of Illumistice. Her time to travel the channels and decide her life path was long over. All of her family and friends remembered their time of travel with fondness and spoke of their experiences often. Journey never said a word about her time. Never. Her life was simple and desolate. She cared, maybe too much, for those she healed. Her heart swelled in response to their pain, but that was all her heart seemed to be capable of. Empathy and then nothing. Her heart was useless to her. Broken beyond all hope.

She woke up minutes before her alarm went off. She kept her eyes closed, waiting. Not waiting for the alarm, but for Redge. His eyes appeared in her mind, sad, and beckoning. She never tired of looking at her memory of his eyes—deep blue green water, the color barely visible over a background of black, like the edges of the sky at sunset before all the light was gone. A shiver rolled through her as she thought of his voice and the message he'd whispered in her mind yesterday, *Journey, I love you. Come back to me. I know it's impossible, come back anyway.*

Every morning at the same time, she heard his plea. For many years she thought she was imagining it. That it was her longing for him that created the whispered words. But then, every so often the words would change. For two years, the message changed from saying *I love you* to *I still love you.* And then there was that terrible month where all he said was, *Journey, please.*

She had no idea how he was sending messages to her. It was impossible, but the messages came every morning, impossible or not.

Journey didn't try to shut him out. She waited for him to whisper to her, and she absorbed every word. It was a soft, sensual torture.

It was her mistake that separated them so many years ago. Her misunderstanding and knee-jerk reaction that had her running from him, magically locking the door behind her as she flew home. It was the one moment she would undo if she could. And it didn't matter how she ached to go back to him. It was forbidden. And she was scared. Scared to break the law. Also terrified to return and find she had imagined his messages all along, and he had found love with someone else, or had possibly found his destined life mate.

Journey held her eyes closed, still waiting. The moment passed. Her alarm sounded. Was he late? He was never late. Not for fifteen years had he missed a day or even been a minute late. She sat up in bed, her heart hammering, her mind immediately jumping to the worst conclusions.

"Alarm off!" she ordered.

The annoying chime quieted.

A sharp-edged chill covered her. She got up and went to shower. The water chased the chill but not the seed of fear that caused it. *Journey, help me.* She gasped as his belated message came into her mind, his voice desperate, broken. Help? How could she possibly help him?

She dried off and dressed quickly, turning on her news screen. She did a search for Regia. It highlighted and popped up in the morning's main headline. Her throat constricted as she read. Illumistice's trade partner was preparing for a many-world takeover. She read the list and found what she hoped she wouldn't. They were on the list. The wizards were planning to invade and conquer Regia.

A sensation she couldn't name solidified inside her. It was something she was sure she had never felt before, and it was absolute in its resolve.

"Lock," she said aloud to her house. "Privacy mode."

A small chime of compliance let her know she would not be interrupted.

Journey sat on her bed and pulled out her channel map from its hidden place. The lines on the fabric paper lit up as she unrolled it. Light moved along the channels open to the youth. The channel to Regia hardly ever lit up anymore. Travel to Regia had become more and more unpopular as civil wars there became more frequent. Illumistice governors closed off channels to worlds they deemed unsafe, or would put them on a limited basis only.

"Come on!" she pleaded with it. "Please!" The light flickered on and off like a dying light bulb. Her heart jumped. It's against the law to go back, she told herself. Her hands shook as she gripped the map. She would lose everything by doing this. Her livelihood, her freedom, her reputation.

Her heart didn't care.

Journey grabbed the thread of light and closed her eyes, breaking the law as she began her travel back to Regia. Back to where her heart lived, back where she'd left it, to do all she could to save the man who kept it. The risk was so great, but still, she set fire to the bridge behind her.

Chapter One

There were moments in Redge's memory that never faded in clarity, or pain. Journey lived at the center of all of them. His heart never let her become the woman of his past. It didn't matter that he hadn't seen her since he was a young man, nor did he have a chance to ever see her again. She was his past, but she was also his present because he never let go of her. He'd tried. After so many long, lonely years, he no longer held out any hope of moving on. Journey, the one, the only woman who ever mattered to him. From the moment love took its first breath, to the current day, she was it for him. And she was gone. His heart was forever full, and her place in his arms would be forever empty.

Redge and Journey didn't make sense in any way whatsoever. They were polar opposites. No to mention they came from different worlds, literally. But the heart knows things, secrets it may never whisper to the head.

Every morning he wrote her a note. Just a few words. Ink and parchment. Then he would burn them. He didn't know why he did this, only that he received some small shred of comfort every time the wisp of smoke disappeared into the air.

Breath filled his lungs, his heart pumped, but his body moved off kilter. He strained against the slave mark on his neck, trying to defy the order pushing him onward. Sweat ran down his face and back and coated him with shame. All these years, since Journey had run away from him, he'd strived to live his life worthy of her good opinion and make up for the sins of his youth. And in this terrible moment, the memory, the worst one, came into sharp focus starting with the look in Journey's jeweled magenta eyes, wide with horror and heartbreak as she witnessed him doing something he'd have given anything to make her un-see.

Journey haunted Redge every day. He'd joined the army to give his life purpose and discipline, and oddly enough to stop the loss of life when he could. He'd never been *just* a soldier. He moved up the ranks for the purpose to create peace and end fighting quickly when fighting was unavoidable. But violence was a major ingredient of his internal makeup, his youth was marked by a short fuse, wild bloodlust, and a need to prove his superiority over his humble beginnings. She'd seen the heart of him, and she'd loved him anyway. She tried to teach him the things that really mattered, but regrettably, he wasn't capable of listening very well back then… In the absence of her, he lived his life for her. A rigid framework of order and reason defined his life and held what was left of the monster inside him in a cage.

Redge never understood what the king had seen in him, or why he was chosen to live in the castle. It was a wonderful turn in the events of his life. His friendship with Syrus had pulled him from the cold loneliness that defined every day since Journey left.

But now, as he moved forward, helpless to stop himself from committing a terrible betrayal of his friends, he saw Journey's eyes, and they condemned him again.

What have I done? What am I doing?

His pulse pushed so hard and fast through his veins. His new slave mark burned hotter, reminding him again he'd been reduced to nothing but a drone; Copernicus' property. His dear friend, Forest, lay at his feet, unconscious. She would come-to quickly; she was tough. He looked down at the magnificent weapon she'd been carrying. Surely, Copernicus knew nothing of this sword, or else his orders would have included bringing it back along with Forest.

Redge picked it up by the carved wooden hilt. He ran over to the edge of the invisible barrier that protected Forest and Syrus' home. He couldn't get through. Quickly, he placed the sword on the ground at the base of a tree and covered it with branches and leaves.

Forest moaned behind him. He ran back to her and bound her hands in front of her with a short length of rope, careful to not tie it too tight so it didn't hurt her, but not so loose she could get out of it. He took her End of the Bridge ring off her hand and slid it onto his own finger. Copernicus wanted it.

Cursing himself and his inability to do anything but what he was told, Redge picked her up. He had to keep his head. He might be a slave, and he was the one to kidnap Forest, but he'd do all he could to protect her until he could get her out again. He tried to keep his mind off Syrus, knowing the pain and horror he was inflicting on his best friend.

Taking one quick glance down at Forest in his arms, Redge pulled in a deep breath, fighting back against the force to obey his orders. The weight of her limp body stung his heart. She was powerful and had a sharp mind, but at the present moment, she seemed so small. He was delivering her to the monster as a prize. Perhaps the prize would be the one to destroy Copernicus. He'd put his faith in Forest.

Forest jolted, her voice ripping through the air in a terrible yell. He tightened his grip on her, wishing his arms would obey his own mind and allow him to turn her loose, but he couldn't. He'd been given an order; he was a slave. Compelled to move forward, he opened a portal and carried her into its opening.

****

Syrus gasped for air as something jerked him from his morning meditation. *Forest.* He stumbled to his feet, trying to breathe. Her heart was screaming. He moved to the window and stuck his head out, his lungs desperately reaching for the air. What was happening to Forest?! What was happening to him? Why couldn't he breathe?

He managed a gulp of air and choked on it. He had to save them! *Them?* His heart felt the racing of Forest's heart, but behind that, there was something, *someone* else's heart. A child… *His* child!

14

An invisible force pushed down on him from overhead. His vision hazed. He saw the attackers dimly from the window: a line of ogres, walking steadily toward the mountain, Devonte, the wizard in the center. A flowing membrane grew on the air, pulsing closer and closer.

Syrus reached out the window, extending his arms as far as they could go. Lightning sparked and snaked over his hands and forearms. Straining with all his might, he pushed it out from himself. Two bolts of red electricity shot, one from each hand, down at the line of attackers coming for them. The red lightning hit the strange wall, fizzling out in sparks against the energy being pushed against the mountain, but he'd ripped a small slit.

Devonte looked up. Syrus ducked the acid green smoke shot at him, and as he lay close to floor, he found he could breathe again.

"Ithiel!" he yelled, praying the master could hear him. "Get down, tell everyone to get down and fight back against the power!"

He crawled to the door. "*Len!*" he shouted for the ogre. "Len, build a portal around the mountain. Push back the force! Everyone, push back! Push back together!"

Guttural yelling filled his ears as the other masters did their best to fight the force descending on them. Syrus rolled to his back, looking up at the ceiling. The momentary relief being close to the floor brought to his lungs, began to ebb. The air grew thicker by the second. Maybe three more breaths, and then he wouldn't be able to breathe again. He opened his mouth, filling his lungs to their full capacity. As he exhaled, his life passed before his eyes. Not his whole life, but the memories that mattered most, down to the most recent passion he and Forest had shared, the moment he knew their child must have been conceived. Then the breath was gone.

Syrus inhaled again, and this time he saw flashes of the present. Forest being attacked, taken away; Regia crying out and dying in smoke and flames. Then the breath was gone. Syrus inhaled again, but this time he saw nothing. He heard the beating of Forest's heart and the racing

15

pulse of their baby in her womb. Nothing had ever convicted him like that sound did in that moment. He held the air in his lungs. He didn't need to breathe. Breathing was overrated.

It was anger that gave him his unique power. There were a few unequivocal moments in his life when he knew his power, felt it grow because of anger: when he transformed from master to mage, when he learned of Forest's slavery, when he killed Lorcan…and when he killed Leith.

What he felt now was something new. Wrath brought him to transcendence. The mingled sound of the beating hearts of those he loved most filled him up. Those individuals who tried to take his loves from him…there would be no pity. No mercy. Strength exploded through him. Whatever titles or attributes he'd previously held melted away.

He was retribution. He was reckoning. He was vengeance.

He stood and walked out of his room. Thinking of Forest's new sword and how he had infused his lightning power inside the black glass of the mountain, he suddenly knew what to do. The stone under his feet awoke and came alive. He moved down deep into the heart of the mountain to the very largest slab of glass that jutted defiantly out of the shadowy rock around it. Syrus placed both his hands flat on the glass. The channels in his palms tore open, forming a connection to the element. He forced his rage into its depths, roaring out his last breath as he poured his power into the glass.

The glass worked as a perfect conductor. Red lightning moved through the entire Obsidian Mountain. It traveled on the veins and cracks to every chunk and shard of glass in the walls. The line of attackers outside stopped dead in their tracks as the black mountain lit up. Lighting ripped through the membrane on the air. In a terrible, blinding flash, they crumpled to the ground, dead. The charred remains of bodies, rock, trees, and scorched earth spanned a fifty foot radius.

All except one. The wizard stood amid the pool of lifeless bodies, tall and defiant. Seemingly immune to Syrus' vengeance. Then, as Syrus exhaled, the wizard wilted in a heap. The convulsions of his body as he wheezed were the only signs he still lived.

The masters followed Syrus out of the mountain, most of them black and coughing. Syrus strode along the line of attackers, sword in hand, making sure they were all dead. He stopped at the crumpled and wheezing Devonte lying face down on the ground.

"Pick him up," Syrus ordered to the masters standing behind him.

Two of them rushed to heft the wizard to his feet. Braced between the two masters, Devonte blinked and squinted at Syrus. A rush of memories came to Syrus as he looked at the wizard who had attended to him years ago when he'd been attacked and lost his sight. So many hours he'd spent with Devonte, who worked, unsuccessfully, to restore his sight. His actions were a sharp stab in Syrus' back. The wizard had always been like a tutor to him. His parents had embraced him and rewarded him for his service and loyalty to the crown, and to Regia. Betrayal and realization that who he *thought* Devonte was and who he really was, were two very different things.

"Syrus…please," he rasped.

Syrus curled his lip at him. "Traitor."

Devonte straightened up a bit, indignation flaring in his eyes at the insult, and spat on the ground. "You're the traitor. You should be sitting on the throne, yet here you are, selfishly pursuing your own interests. Instead of taking a queen from the appointed bloodlines, you rut with that Halfling… And now look at you…you look like some kind of… monster."

"That's right." Syrus' voice went deadly calm. "I am now."

"You've been pushing the boundaries of your ability." Devonte looked around at the dead ogres lying on the ground and then back at Syrus. "You did that, didn't you? You've become a killer. I'm ashamed of you."

"*You're* ashamed of *me*? You come here, leading an unprovoked attack. You've joined with Copernicus, who kills without conscience. Kills whole villages of women and children."

"If you kill me, you're just as bad as he is."

Syrus threw his head back and laughed, a terrible laugh that placed fear in those around him. "Pathetic fallacy." He nodded to the masters holding Devonte. "Turn him loose. We'll end this with combat."

They let go.

Devonte grabbed the one on his right, using him as shield, his hand at the young master's throat. "All of you get back, or I'll kill him!"

A spark snapped on Devonte's index finger. He backed up, towing the terrified master with him. Syrus walked slowly after them.

"Get back!" Devonte yelled.

"You and Copernicus threaten and take the lives of those who cannot fight back. Of those who did nothing to you." Syrus reached out his hand. Electricity swirled in his palm and shot through the air into Devonte's eye. The wizard fell to the ground, smoke coming from his ears, eyes, mouth, and nose. The young master scurried to the side, his terrified gaze darting between Devonte and Syrus.

Syrus leaned over Devonte and checked for a pulse. A weak thump pushed under his finger. He straightened and thrust his sword through the wizard's heart.

He turned to the young man standing next to him, handed him the sword, and clapped him on the shoulder. "There's a vast difference between killing and murder. Never forget that."

The young man nodded quickly.

Syrus walked back to the group of masters, all of them watching him intently. "I have to go... They've taken Forest."

The entire group looked up as a line of black smoke snaked over the pale sun.

"It appears they've taken more than that. There's death in the air," Ithiel said. "We're going with you."

Syrus nodded. "You are all masters of the Blood Kata. You know what that means? Deadly bastards, every one of you. This is personal. Not just for me. Regia is *our* world. Now it's time for us to defend it. Pull no punches. The insurgents must be crushed. Leave no traces of this poison, so it can harm no one else. Are you ready?"

A roar of assent rose up from the group.

"Let's go. We make for Halussis."

****

Shi raised her eyes to the sky and watched the smoke drift over the tops of the trees. How long had it been since she'd truly felt despair? Really felt it as she did now? Would the whole world perish around her while she could do nothing except listen to their screams and smell their deaths on the wind? The Wood was her prison.

She looked back at the Heart and tried to force herself to be numb. Just yesterday, the flames were gray. Regia's heart had been healing. The color of the flames of the manifestation grew lighter by small degrees every day. But now…now all progress was reversed. The Heart burned black again. The breeze moving the leaves of the crystal trees chimed a tune of death and rage. Shi had never heard the likes of it before.

She wrapped her branchy arms around herself. Was Forest still alive? Her mind spun on *what ifs*. Her ghostly heart flipped in panic at the terrible scenarios her mind created. Shi broke into tiny pieces inside. She needed to be grounded. There was only one person who could help her now. *Am I ready?*

She moved slowly to her trunk, the wood long petrified, all the blush of life drained as colorless as glass. So long, she had caged Ler

19

here. And never had she interacted with him beyond the occasional brush of her hand on the cold bark. Perhaps her anger was finally spent.

Hesitating, she clenched and unclenched her fingers. Her hand rested against the crystal bark, but she kept it on the exterior, not allowing her hand to slide within. He stirred and rose up to the surface. His face came into view from inside her trunk. He placed his hand against hers. Shi gasped and pulled her hand back. *No, not yet...not yet.*

His eyes went sad, he turned away, and began to fade back into the trunk's depths.

"Wait!" she called.

If she freed him, Death would surely come back and take his soul where it was meant to be.

Impossible tears stung her eyes as she placed both of her hands back on the bark. *Leramiun,* her heart groaned. Shi slid into her trunk, her spirit crossing the barrier she created between them for the first time in ten thousand years.

He looked just the same as he had the day she bound herself to him and became his queen. Shi glided into his open arms. As soon as they touched, her flesh shimmered, shivered, and pulled back into the shape she used to be. She sighed soul deep. Ler felt solid to her, and she felt solid against him. Perhaps their souls were made of the same fabric after all. He held her in silence. Love detained and dormant for so long, trembled.

Chapter Two

Forest held still, her hands loosely bound together in her lap. She could have easily slipped out of the tie but she decided against it, for the moment. The back of her head throbbed, but she'd suffered worse. Cold sweat pushed out of her pores as her heart pumped pure adrenaline instead of blood through her body. Electric currents snapped and flashed inside her, making it difficult to maintain her resolve to calm down and be still. Her breath was hot and moist in the confines of the fabric hood. She desperately needed fresh air.

Syrus' spirit echoed across whatever distance parted them. He knew she was gone. His agony and desperation flooded into her chest. There were no reassuring sensations she could send back to him. She knew nothing of her location or the fate that awaited her. She remained motionless, waiting, calculating.

Syrus and Rahaxeris would come for her. That was comforting. Who could stand against their combined ire? Still, she wasn't the type to do nothing and wait for the cavalry to show up. She would draw upon anything and everything she could to survive, to escape, no matter how pathetic or underhanded the means might be.

An aftershock from the quickening vibrated in her lower abdomen. Forest gritted her teeth and held the cry of pain deep inside her lungs. No one knew she was pregnant, and she intended to keep it that way. *Little Secret, you're safe inside me. I'll protect you.*

She leaned her head against the hard surface behind her. It felt as though she'd been propped up in a corner. Redge had been the one to kidnap her. That thought was a lifeline. No matter where she was or what she was up against, she already had an ally. He'd had good reason to do what he did. She didn't believe for a second that he was on *their* side. But where was he now?

The floor under her butt was solid, but she felt a rocking. Was that just the effects of the blow to her head? Her stomached ached and rolled with nausea. She would *not* throw up in this fabric bag! The whole room lurched. She couldn't stand it any longer. Despite her resolve to be perfectly still, Forest raised her bound hands and pulled at the hood until it came off.

It was a cell, totally bare. A perfect box. The walls, ceiling, and floor were all the same dull bronze color. She touched the wall next to her with the back of her hand. It was cold and metallic. There was a door on the opposite wall, but it had no knob or handle; all she could see was the outline. The light overhead came from a small circle and reminded her of the skylights she'd seen in the *Rune-dy's* headquarters deep under Kyhael. And as she looked closer, she realized it was much the same. The light coming through the ceiling was sunlight.

Forest rubbed her bound wrists together and smiled. Redge had done that on purpose, she was certain. She could slip the ties when she wanted. It didn't really matter how tight or loose he'd tied her, all she had to do was shift her wrists a little smaller to get out. The rope slid off into her lap. She pocketed it.

Forest stood just as the room pitched sideways again, knocking her off balance and into the wall. She spread her legs a little farther apart than her shoulders to gain more balance. It was as if she was on a swing...or the water. Forest strained her ears but heard nothing. She knelt and pressed her ear against the floor. Sure enough, she heard the lapping sound of waves. She closed her eyes and cursed Copernicus for being too clever.

She rolled onto her back and stared up at the small skylight, swamped with despair. She held everything inside. She thought of the Fair. Were all her friends dead? Just like the shifter colony? Had they all died because Copernicus knew they were a way to strike at her? Had it always been about her? If so, why? Why did she matter so damn much to him? So many faces flashed before her eyes, friends, family, even past enemies who might now be dead. Why did Copernicus want to break her? He could just kill her.

She closed her eyes and pressed her hands to her lower abdomen, listening to the child's pulse. Her heart reached out for Syrus. Could he feel the baby? Did he know?

"Oh, my love…" she whispered. "Help me, Syrus…What should I do? How do I get back to you?"

His eyes loomed in her mind. She drew strength from their depths. Syrus pulled his power from anger. Her anger usually clouded her judgment and made her sloppy. He turned his rage into a weapon, but he always had control over it. How could she do that? How could she be more like him? Syrus could create spheres, she'd seen it… That's what she'd do, mentally at least.

Forest imagined a glass sphere in her chest. She took everything she was feeling and poured it all into that empty vessel. She would hold it in silence, buried deep inside, until the time came to break it open and empty out her contempt in its purified rancor over Copernicus. She'd pour out every last drop until he was utterly destroyed and his dead body was nothing but ashes dancing on the wind.

Approaching footsteps had her jumping to her feet, her heart thundering in her ears. She took a deep breath and blew it out slowly, trying to force her pulse to steady. *Is this it? Am I about to die?*

The door swung open. Redge entered, followed by two others. As soon as she saw Redge, she cast her gaze elsewhere so no one would be able to see that she knew him. The other two men were identical except one was shorter and slightly less bulky. The shorter one pulled out Forest's old silver sword and smiled at her tauntingly. She recognized him, now. This was Shreve, the shifter she'd fought at Fortress, who could shift across sexes. She turned her gaze away from him and looked up into the face of her enemy, Copernicus.

He was at least a head taller than Syrus and almost twice as thick. His honey wheat hair was cropped short over a square but surprisingly handsome face. His almond shaped eyes were a layered, muddy hazel, and his full mouth curved into a terrifying oversized smile as he looked down at her. Forest didn't know what she expected, but she could see a madness inside him. It was not unlike what she'd seen with Netriet when the shadow lived inside her, amplified times ten. Copernicus' face and body were the lid on a vault containing a jumble of horrors and confusion. His gaze ate her up inch by inch, and he guarded none of the emotions coming from his eyes.

Forest lifted her head and squared her shoulders defiantly. Copernicus laughed, a delighted throaty chuckle, and swooped down on her. She had nowhere to evade. His massive arms lifted her off the ground. She held herself rigid, her mind stumbling. Copernicus didn't crush her, or try to break her back, nor did he attempt to assault her sexually. He hugged her like a precious, long lost friend.

"Sister," he whispered in her ear as he kissed the side of her head. "At long last...we are together."

He set her back on her feet, but he was still forcibly in her personal space. He touched her cheek and combed his fingers through her hair. She was shaking inside, but she continued to hold herself still.

"So beautiful…Shreve, you didn't tell me how beautiful she was."

"I told you she was beautiful, Father," Shreve argued.

"You didn't describe her. You were vague. Look at those eyes! See the banked rage beneath the green?"

Shreve shrugged. "She's a shifter. She'll look different in an hour."

Copernicus sighed and rolled his eyes. "What about you, Redge? Don't you think Forest is beautiful?"

"Yes. Very."

"See now, Redge has taste."

Forest looked carefully at everything she could see. She filed every nuance into her mind: body language, tone of voice, anything that gave her clues about her captors.

"Sister?" she chanced speaking.

Copernicus didn't take his eyes off her as he spoke to the others. "Shreve, you can go. Redge, leave us for a moment, but stay just outside the door."

He waited for the others to leave and the door to close. His expression was mild, but his eyes continued to devour her.

"Relax, Forest. I can practically hear your heart beating, despite how you're working to hide it."

"You called me, sister."

"And that amazes you? You *are* my sister. We share the same father."

He paused, Forest assumed for effect. It could be true. She still didn't know that much about Rahaxeris, but she knew enough to know it could be true.

"That's why I'm here, isn't it? It's not about me, it's about him."

"Double threat, smart and beautiful…maybe that's what you've got that compels men's hearts."

"I am more than that."

Copernicus' smile turned into a sneer. "Yes, I can see you are many things. A little arrogant, too. I hate arrogance."

He moved so fast, she didn't even have time to flinch. His massive fist slammed into her face. Stars and colors exploded behind her eyes as she flew backward into the wall. She shook her head and pinched the bridge of her bleeding nose. He didn't strike again. When her vision cleared, she had to blink a few times to make sure she was really seeing what she was seeing.

Tears clouded his eyes, and his face crumpled. He wrung his massive hands over and over. "I'm so sorry, sister. Please forgive me."

His unnatural behavior alarmed her more than anything else. She had to play him, despite how dangerous a prospect that was.

She rubbed the blood running from her nose across her cheek purposefully. "You hurt me, brother."

"I'm sorry," he said again. "Oh, your face. Your gorgeous face. It'll heal without notice, I'm sure."

"What is it you want from me? How can I help you?"

"I want our family to be together, but that is a personal desire. There is a grave threat coming. It might not look like it, but everything I have done since coming home to Regia has been to protect and serve."

Forest bit down on her tongue as she thought of all the people he'd killed. The faces of the dead cried out to her. She eased the memory back and tucked her vengeance away. She had to play along.

"I don't think I can do this," he muttered. "I love you too much... You have no idea how much I love you, Forest. But you must be shown. You're wild. You must be broken."

Shit, I don't like the sound of this. Forest thought.

"I have questions." she scrambled. "You need to tell me about this new danger to Regia."

He smiled again. "I will. I can see that you're scared. You're like a child without boundaries. First, you must learn trust. I have put you in an invisible circle, and you will stay inside it."

"I don't understand."

26

"You will...Redge, come back in here," he shouted.

Redge returned. He looked anxiously at Forest for a split second and then turned his eyes to the floor. Copernicus wrapped his hulking arm around Redge's shoulders.

"I love this guy. So strong, so dedicated to me. It wasn't always that way. But you know that, don't you? He used to work for you, didn't he?"

"I don't know what you're talking about." Her voice was flat.

"Come now. I know the two of you know each other. Redge has spilled his guts to me—under duress, of course. He didn't have a choice, but still."

She looked hard at Redge; she could see it. The signs were there. His shoulders hung in defeat, and he continued to stare at the floor.

"You see, sister? He's my slave, as are *almost* all of my followers."

The urge to attack Copernicus swelled inside her, but she knew she couldn't win. She had to protect her baby. But her heart broke for Redge. She knew what it was like to be a slave, to have no control over your own actions.

"So, I have things to do, and my heart is apparently too soft for you, sister, to take you in hand the way you need it. I'm going to have your old friend Redge do the dirty work for me."

"What?!" she demanded.

Copernicus ignored her and turned Redge to face him. "I'm giving you an order, Redge. You are to beat her within an inch of her life. You will not stop or show her mercy until she is in a state that will take even a fast healer like her considerable time to recover from. Do you understand?"

"Yes, my lord." Redge's voice broke, and his muscles gave a little jerk in response to the order.

"Good." Copernicus turned to leave. "Oh, and you better not scar her beautiful face."

The door shut behind Redge. He advanced on her. Forest placed both of her hands on her stomach and mouthed the word *baby*. His eyes rounded and flooded with pain, but he nodded as his hands came up and fisted.

He swung. She ducked, coming up behind him and shoved him into the wall. He spun around and kicked out, sweeping her feet out from under her. Forest landed on her back, the fall knocking the wind out of her. She gasped and cried out as he kicked her hip. The bone fractured under the force. He wasn't capable of pulling back under Copernicus' order.

Forest slammed her elbow into the side of his knee, knocking him off balance. As he stumbled, she grabbed his leg and pulled him off his feet. He landed on the floor next to her.

"I'm sorry," he wheezed. "I'm in over my head."

"I know. I forgive you."

It was terrible. They were friends, and now they were turned on each other like puppets on strings. She didn't want to hurt him, just as he didn't want to hurt her.

Redge roared as he tried to fight back his compulsion to obey Copernicus' order. Forest pulled herself up just as he jumped on her, pinning her down and wrapping his hands around her throat. His tears fell on her face as she tried to pry his hands off.

"Tell me what to do, Forest," he begged as he pressed down harder on her windpipe, making it impossible for her to answer.

She brought her knee up, smashing his groin. He fell off her, compressing into the fetal position, groaning.

Her first breath burned like fire all the way down her throat and through her lungs. Tears scalded her eyes. She rolled and tried to get up, but her broken hip screamed in stabbing pain and kept her down. She panted, sweat sliding down her forehead, as she looked over at Redge. There was no way out of this. She could keep fighting, but all that would do was hurt Redge and further endanger her baby.

She thought of her child as she wrestled back her nature to fight. Her nature clawed and raged. Maternal instinct reared up and shoved the wildness down with authority. Forest pulled her body tight around her stomach and waited. She heard Redge get to his feet, but she didn't look at him. She closed her eyes tight. *I'll protect you, Little Secret.*

He punched her in the side, his fist breaking her ribs. All the breath was pushed out of her, and she struggled to inhale again. He kicked her ruthlessly; her undamaged hip broke like the other. Her knees fractured under his boots. Forest became dizzy, the pain spinning her, and her stomach lurched with nausea. *Protect the baby. Protect the baby.* She focused on her child, trying to shut out the agony and the nightmare of the cause.

The force of his blows bruised her all the way into her internal organs. He continued to hit her over and over. Her blood splattered the walls and ran like a river over the floor. She'd never felt pain like this, pain that warned of swift approaching death. Her body broke, but still she used it to protect her baby. Finally...finally the onslaught stopped.

Forest tried to open her burning eyes. Redge leaned over her, covered in sweat and her blood. He touched the top of her head gently.

"It's over now, the order has lifted," he whispered. "Will you be all right? Please tell me you'll survive."

She jerked her head forward once.

"Tell me what to do?"

Her voice came out quiet and disjointed, her throat bubbling with blood. "Tell Syrus I love him."

29

Sweet unconsciousness wrapped its loving arms around her and took her into the deep dark where all she could hear was the beating heart of her child.

****

Redge winced as Copernicus dug his fingers into his shoulder, smiling as he inflicted pain.

"Tell me, what was it like to hurt her? The truth, please."

Redge ground his teeth together, trying not to answer. The words came out anyway. "One of the worst… moments of my whole life."

Copernicus stopped digging in his fingers and patted him on the back instead. "I envy you such a moment, Redge. Those incidents that pepper life and change who we are. You know what I mean." He tapped Redge's forehead with his index finger. "You were one way yesterday, and now, there's a new twist in there."

Copernicus turned his back on Redge and paced a few times in front of him. Apprehension saturated Redge's insides as he waited for his master to come to whatever diabolical conclusion he was mulling over.

Copernicus turned back to Redge and looked him in the eyes. "Tell me what would be the worst thing I could make you do right now?"

Redge shook his head, clamping his mouth shut. His jaw immediately began shaking with the effort to keep silent. Copernicus snorted and pushed on Redge's slave mark, like a button. Shredding, burning poison seemed to move through him from his master's touch, and he answered the damn question.

"Send me away, so I can't watch over Forest."

"Ah, yes. I see. Grand job you've done so far though, huh? She's here because you brought her, she's in there, bloodied and fighting for her life, injured by your hands. You can't protect her from me. She's

30

mine." Copernicus' eyes glinted as he held out his hand. "Give me Forest's portal ring."

Redge obeyed.

Copernicus wrapped his fingers over the ring. A black portal opened behind him. "You will never see Forest again in this life. Remember her, remember the way she looked as you beat her. I'm sending you back to Halussis. Keep to yourself. Contact no one from your old life. Do not attempt to associate with my other slaves. Wait for your orders. Shreve will come to you soon. Goodbye, Redge."

The orders sank into his blood and bones like an infection. Copernicus pushed Redge into the portal. He fell on the ground at the other end, as the portal discarded him. For a few moments, he just lay there, with no will to move ever again. When he did finally stand up and look around, he saw he was on the edge of Halussis.

Let me wake from this horror. The air felt too heavy. He didn't want to breathe anymore. Forest's blood was dried on his hands. He'd hurt her badly, so badly. How had he done it? He'd been turned into a torture device and used against his friend. And she was pregnant! Self-hatred blossomed all through him, solidified, and became absolute. He thought of Syrus. He might have just killed his best friend's unborn child! How could he ever look him in the eyes again?

Why couldn't he fight the order, at least a little? At least enough to pull his punches? Why wasn't he strong enough to push back? A concrete feeling of worthlessness settled in his stomach. He had been so stupid. So arrogant to believe he could infiltrate the enemy. The sensation of his knuckles hammering through her skin, muscles, and bone vibrated deep in his hands. Tears welled in his eyes. He would never forget even the smallest detail of this day. Each sensory experience pushed a needle through the outer membrane of his heart, just deep enough to bleed, so he couldn't ignore it. But not deep enough to lose the feeling and grow numb.

31

Redge hated everything about himself, and he was sure the hatred would never go away, never ease, or lose its clarity. Journey's eyes came into his mind, filled with accusation and tears.

His eyes fell on the outline of the Onyx Castle in the distance. It had been his home most of his life, but no more. He couldn't imagine ever setting foot there again. Where could he go? His orders were to stay in Halussis and keep to himself. He had one place to go. A place he'd never wanted to see since he'd left it in his youth. His father's house. Well, it was no worse than he deserved.

Redge turned from looking at the heart of the city and headed away. At least the old stone house was in the rural outskirts of the city. If he was all alone, then he couldn't hurt anyone else. His feet found the path without conscious direction from his brain. It twisted along, the desert giving way to wild growth. Entropy had claimed the area. None of the neighbors he remembered from his childhood remained. Their homes were reduced to piles of rubble. The whole area was abandoned.

Redge gazed at the home of his youth at the end of the path. It was a ruin. The roof was broken in over three fourths of the house. Vines snaked through the windows. One large tree grew in the corner and up through the roof. The stones had turned green and purple with moss and lichen. He looked down. This was exactly the spot where he had killed his father. He spat on the ground, and the memory and continued forward. The doorway of the house yawned like the mouth of a monster, ready to swallow him.

His father's voice sounded in his head as he remembered with acute clarity the night he lost his heart.

"I know all about it, boy. Did you think I wouldn't find out?" his father snarled.

"It's none of your business who I love. It's my life."

32

"I won't have it, Redge! You're already a laughingstock. Vampires mate vampires. You will not taint our family's bloodline with another race. Not only is she not a vampire, she's not even a Regian!"

"I don't care what you or anyone else says. I love her."

The uppercut to his chin caught Redge off guard. His vision flashed black for a moment, the pain shockingly sharp. His father had never hit him that hard before. He rotated his jaw and blinked a few times, making sure his feet were solid on the ground.

His father rubbed his knuckles and squinted through bloodshot, drunken eyes. Redge sucked in a breath and pulled himself up to his full height. He'd tried to keep Journey a secret from his father. He'd known it would be like this. He'd known the moment his father discovered their love, Redge would be forced to make some tough choices. Choices meant for men, and he could barely call himself that.

He regarded his father. The weight in the air was suffocating. He wouldn't give Journey up. This was the hill he would die on. His life was trash, had always been trash, until her. She was air and light and life. But now, what could he do? He had no real profession—the sleazy drug running his father had tried to train him in, didn't count. And he'd given that up in any case.

"Fine. I can see there's no compromise here. I'm leaving."

His father beat him to the door, blocking his path. "You're not going anywhere. You're my son, and you'll do what I say! And I say you'll never see her again."

Redge fisted one hand and punched his father in the jaw, exactly the same way he'd just been punched. His father slammed back into the door and fell to the ground. Redge leaned down and attempted to drag him out of the way. He reared up and grabbed Redge around the back of the neck, sinking his fangs into his shoulder. Crying out in pain, Redge flailed and struck at his father until he shook him off.

"I'm not going to stop. You won't get out of here in time. I know she's coming here to see you tonight." His father smiled through his blood-coated fangs. "I've been following you two. I know your patterns. I know all about how she sneaks over here. She's on her way here right now, isn't she?"

All the blood drained from Redge's face, and his breath hitched in his lungs. She was on her way to meet him.

"I'm putting an end to this tonight, boy. I can see you're going to be stubborn...I guess I'll just have to kill her."

"No!" His voice came out in a strangled rasp.

His father chuckled. "I've killed before, you know I have. I can't say I really enjoyed it, but tonight, who knows? She does have a most agreeable neck, I'll give you that, boy. It might feel good to strangle her. I don't know anyone else who's killed a Storyteller. This will make me notorious."

"You're full of hot air, old man." Redge pushed out bravado he didn't feel. "You wouldn't hurt her."

"Wouldn't I?"

"No, you wouldn't. Storytellers are sacred. You'd never get away with it. I'd tell everyone. They'd drain you dry and burn your blood in the city square."

His father got to his feet, smiling. "You're the one full of hot air. Wait...I think I hear her coming up the path right now. Don't go anywhere, Redge. I want you to see this."

His father pulled open the door. In the distance, Redge could see Journey's silhouette under the cast of moonlight. The sound of metal scraping cut through his soul as his father pulled out the knife he kept on his belt. Redge's vision tunneled around her as his heart beat like a war drum in his ears. He couldn't let her die, but could he stop his father? He was on the edge of losing something precious, and he was out of time deciding which was worth more to him. His father was an asshole, but he was his father, the only family he had. But Journey was the keeper of his soul. He'd handed it over to her whole, keeping none of it for himself.

He imagined it all before anything happened. He saw his father run her down and stab her. He heard her screams echo through the stars. She cried out his name...

There were no thoughts, no strategy. Redge moved as though he had transformed into a machine. Gears and clockwork just doing what they were designed to do. It was all a blur of hands, blood, cries, pain, and death.

It was so much worse than he could have ever imagined. Breaking, taking life like that, with his hands. So sensory, so long, so personal. And when it was over, Redge looked up from his father's dead body into Journey's eyes. She was unharmed, but the hideous measures it took to keep her that way lay at her feet.

He'd done what he had to, to save her. But now, all the love he used to see in her eyes drained away, replaced by disbelief and fear. He'd never seen anything so clearly. In the process of being her hero, he had become a monster instead. If only she hadn't witnessed him killing his father, he could have made her understand he'd only done what he had to protect her.

He reached out. "Journey..."

She shook her head and stepped back. He grasped her by the shoulders with his blood-soaked hands. She screamed as though the blood on her golden-brown skin burned. Tears ran down her cheeks.

"I had to protect you..."

A terrible stillness came over her. She closed her eyes and took a slow breath. When she opened her eyes again, they were flat. She pressed her lips to his, placing both of her hands on his face. Her kiss was a brutal goodbye. She shoved away from him and ran.

35

"Journey!"

He started after her, but she reached into the air as she ran, catching a hold of something he couldn't see. Then it sparked gold in her hand, burning his eyes. Then she sparked too and was absorbed into the golden light stream. He would never see her again, and where she'd gone, he couldn't follow.

****

Syrus, with his band of masters, arrived at his and Forest's cottage. They all stood back and left him alone as he looked around at the site where Forest had been abducted. His sharp eyes picked up tiny details, and he followed the footprints of her kidnapper to the bracken covering her sword. An audible gasp broke from the masters watching as Syrus pulled the sword out and held it up.

He walked over to Ithiel. "Whoever took her took the time to hide her sword. How does that add up?" Ithiel asked.

A tiny seed germinated in Syrus' mind… Could it have been Redge? He thought back to the message Redge sent that Forest shared with him. Redge was undercover. Who else would leave the sword behind? But why would he take Forest at all? Why couldn't he protect her, lead the enemy away from her? Perhaps he was totally off. Maybe Forest had hidden her sword. But that didn't tally either. Forest would never lay down her weapon and leave herself defenseless.

Why had Forest left the protection of their home? What drew her out? Syrus looked up. The air hung heavy with the smell of death. He drew it into his nose. It came from the direction of the Fair.

Syrus looked at the group. "On your guard…follow me."

36

Chapter Three

Syrus stood at the entrance of the Fair. The wall around the tiny community was now the equivalent of a fence around a cemetery. Every building and structure was reduced to twisted, charred remains. The dead lay in a row off to the side, in a large pile. Two figures worked furiously, hunched over, digging graves.

Syrus approached the closest one. "Hey."

The man started. A blade blurred through the air toward Syrus' head. He dodged, just barely, impressed at the man's speed. His face was soot and tear-streaked, his eyes held tight around his grief. Syrus recognized him.

"Merick, it's me, Syrus."

Merick's eyes cleared a little, and recognition filled them. He fell onto his knees next to the open grave beside him. "They're all dead. My friends…they never did anything to deserve this. My best friend, Tek. His loving mate, Martia. They're dead. Why?"

The other gravedigger came up beside Merick and placed a gentle hand on his shoulder. Netriet's face was likewise covered in tear-streaked soot. A terrible expression crossed her features as she looked at Syrus. Confused, as though she recognized him, but didn't. She tried to cover her reaction, but then she gasped as her eyes fell on Forest's sword. She reached out and grabbed Syrus by the forearm, her eyes wide and beseeching.

"Forest? She wasn't in this, was she? Is she all right? I haven't seen her... uh… among the dead here."

Syrus' throat was thick. "She wasn't here, but she was… taken."

37

Netriet's eyes widened and filled with pity. He looked away from her.

"How is it that everyone here died except you two?"

"We weren't here!" Merick threw his shovel on the ground roughly. "We were coming to visit. We heard their cries from a distance and"—he broke off, shouting a string of curses—"by the time we got here, we were too late to save anyone."

Merick picked his shovel back up and began digging again.

Syrus narrowed his eyes and surveyed the scene.

"There's not much to learn here, I'm afraid," Netriet said. "Our friends are laid out there." She pointed at the row of bodies. "The insurgents are in the pile over there. We were about to burn them."

"You caught none of them?"

She shook her head gravely. "There were only three left when we arrived. We didn't ask questions. Merick killed two of them. The last one suffered great pain, compliments of my alien arm, before he died... What are you going to do?" she asked Syrus.

"We are going to Halussis, to the Onyx Castle. To organize, so we can strike back."

"We'll help," she said, then she looked at Merick. "Right?"

Merick paused in his furious shoveling and sighed. "I'm going to finish this."

"We will meet you there," she said, moving over next to Merick and shoveling with him.

****

Halussis was in chaos and panic in the aftermath of the strike. A small relief came on Syrus as he and the masters arrived. The loss of life was minimal compared to the annihilation of the Fair. People moved aside in fear and awe as Syrus passed. He didn't have time to dwell on their reactions—he had no idea how terrifying he looked. He moved apart, like some vengeful elemental or angel of death. Blackened hands, charred robes, the light in his eyes matching the lightning in the sword he carried.

The massive double doors of the Onyx castle hung broken and askew on their hinges. Lazy tendrils of smoke curled from some of the windows. Syrus' heart clenched preemptively as he pushed into the main entrance, afraid of what he would find. Had he lost his father today, as well?

Bodies lined the walls.

The sounds of Zeren's voice, giving orders, drifted down the hall and had Syrus sighing in relief. Ogres carried bodies away from the throne room. Zeren's cheek was cut and bleeding, and he held his left arm strangely against his body. Otherwise, he looked fine.

"Father."

Zeren's head whipped around. He rushed over and grabbed Syrus in a tight one-armed hug.

"Are you all right? I've had reports of an attack on the Obsidian Mountain." Zeren let go and looked closely at his son, worry creasing his forehead. "What happened to you? You're changed."

Syrus gestured to the group of masters behind him. "We were attacked by a band of ogres led by Devonte. But that doesn't matter now."

"What does matter, then?"

Syrus moved his father away from anyone close by and lowered his voice. "Forest's been kidnapped."

Zeren gritted his teeth in fury.

"It's worse than that, Father... She's pregnant."

He touched Syrus on the chest. "Can you feel her? Is she all right, for now at least?"

Syrus nodded. "I feel her heartbeat, and the child's, but I'm getting nothing else."

"Listen to me, son. We've learned a lot about our enemy today. Every one of the insurgents who attacked the castle today were slaves."

"Slaves?"

Zeren nodded. "All but one. The first insurgents anyone apprehended were all believers. Even the ones Forest caught, right?"

"Yes."

"We killed a bunch today, twenty five, give or take, and all had slave marks... They're just drones following orders."

Syrus looked down, running a hand through his hair. "This changes things, damn it. Now we can't just kill them all. They're victims, too. Copernicus is clever."

"We'll figure this out, together. And we'll get Forest back."

****

Copernicus sat on the floor next to Forest and watched her. Her unconscious breathing was labored as her body fought to heal from her beating. He smoothed the hair off her face. Her complexion was pallid and clammy. He could see the veins in her eyelids. He debated moving her to his bed. No, she was a prisoner. Her discomfort was part of the process.

The blood on her face bothered him. He got up and left, only to return a few moments later with a bowl of clean water and a soft rag. Copernicus bathed her face gently. She moaned in pain but didn't wake. He crawled on top of her, covering her with his body, but not letting one inch of himself press down on her. He looked at her under him and surrendered to his emotions. Love, as he had never felt before, and then hate in equal measures.

"I hate you. What makes you so damn special? Why does Father love you and not me? Why do *I* love you? *Why*?!"

Forest didn't even flinch against his yelling. Her face remained smooth, her eyes closed. He leaned down and pressed his lips against hers. For a moment, he pretended she kissed him back, and he sucked on her lips. He was never giving her up, no matter what deal he made with Rahaxeris. Forest was his.

His vampire side came out, and he was seized with the urge to bite her. To take a drink and see what he could learn about what lay inside her through the taste of her blood. His teeth ached as he inhaled at the vein in her neck. He buried his face against her softness. His fangs sank through the lovely membrane of her skin, hot blood flowing into his mouth. He rolled the liquid life around his tongue. *Well, now, what's this I taste? How can she have vampire in her blood?*

A knock at the door jarred him back to reality, and he pulled his mouth back from her neck and wiped the back of his hand over his lips.

"Father? I'm back. Are you in there?"

Copernicus opened the door and stepped out of the cell. "Let's go out on the deck. I need some fresh air."

The sunset moved through the sky and reflected off the surface of the water. Copernicus rested his elbows on the ship's railing and took a deep breath, clearing his mind of Forest.

"So…how did our strike go?"

Shreve scowled out at the water. "Everything went according to plan, or as close as can be hoped for. We lost quite a few in the hit on the Onyx castle. The Fair was completely annihilated. We, umm…lost all of the ogres and Devonte at the Mountain. No idea what happened there as

41

no one was left to tell the tale… Our time is running out, Father. All the masters have gone to Halussis and are joining forces with Zeren. One of our believers told me he saw Syrus from a distance, and that he…"

Copernicus turned his full attention onto Shreve. "He what?"

"He said Syrus looks like a god. Like some kind of lightning god of vengeance with a lightning bolt encased in a huge black sword."

Copernicus raised his eyebrows. "Interesting. Don't go out of your way, but if you get the chance to see him yourself, I'd like a detailed account of that. What else did you learn?"

"Nothing. A lot of innocent life was lost today. Powerful forces will be coming down on us very soon, so I hope you're ready with the next step, or we're all dead."

"Don't be weak, boy. Phase two is ready to go." He pulled a wax-sealed letter out of his shirt and handed it to Shreve. "Deliver this to Rahaxeris."

Shreve sighed. "I guess if I don't come back you'll know he killed me. Do you have a plan B?"

Copernicus laughed and handed Shreve Forest's portal ring. "I don't need one. He will come with you willingly."

"If you're so sure"—Shreve thrust the letter back—"take it to him yourself."

Copernicus' eyes narrowed. "Do I need to punish you? Why are you insubordinate? If I go to the *Rune-dy*, I will never make it out alive… Have some compassion, Shreve. I was born in that place. The next time I set foot there, it will be to burn it to ashes… No. The time is not right for me. For the plan to work, it has to be you."

"Fine, but I expect a reward for this."

Copernicus raised one eyebrow and smirked. "A reward? What reward do you want?"

"I want time alone with Forest."

"Time alone to do what exactly?"

"That's my business, and no questions will be part of the reward."

Copernicus turned his face away from Shreve, his complexion coloring red in anger, and his jaw clenching. "I won't say yes or no right now. Bring me Rahaxeris, and I'll consider it."

Shreve rolled the ring around in his hand and opened a portal, resigned to playing messenger boy. He shifted into the form of an elf before stepping into it. He'd listened to Copernicus rant about Rahaxeris his whole life, but he had never actually seen him. Shreve was sure the high priest wouldn't live up to the hype. But the moment was pivotal for him. He was about to set eyes on the creator. Copernicus' most loved, worshiped, talked about, and hated entity. Rahaxeris was everything to Copernicus. Shreve hoped Rahaxeris would come as predicted. He wasn't ready to die just yet. And delivering the *Rune-dy* meant Shreve had done something Copernicus couldn't.

The portal dumped him on a side street in Kyhael, behind a building, where luckily, no one had seen his arrival. He straightened and looked around. A terrible weight fell into his stomach, and the letter in his hand burned his skin. He breathed heavily. This wasn't the first time he'd felt like this. It was like being sick. Like his spirit hated his flesh and no longer fit properly inside the confines of his body. In the last few days, every time he looked at the dead, or heard screams of pain, or the tears of the grieving, he felt like this.

He was sorry. Guilty. But what did he do about it? Nothing. He perpetuated the misery.

Shreve shook himself, trying to dislodge the sensation and make it go away. He had a job to do. He wanted to please his father. He looked at the letter in his hand and scowled. Both he and Copernicus had daddy

43

issues. The guilt slunk into the background, but it didn't go away as he headed toward the center of Kyhael.

****

Copernicus tried to focus on what lay ahead of him. Not just for the rest of his journey to the throne, but for the rest of the day. Today was more important than anything else. Rahaxeris would come. He would finally see his father again. He would finally get the answers he needed.

And he would begin the process of slowly pulling the razor-edged thread of revenge around and around Rahaxeris until it wound around his neck and cut off his head.

But his swirling thoughts continued to be eclipsed by his curiosity of what he'd tasted in Forest's blood. It might be important that he know before Rahaxeris came. He didn't want to be the one missing a crucial piece of knowledge that could tip the scales in any way other than the direction he wanted them to tip. The fact that her blood was sweet, and his throat burned with the desire for more had nothing to do with it. Nothing whatsoever.

He knelt back down beside her, burning with the desire to bite her again. Why would she have vampire in her blood? Was everything he'd learned about her wrong, and she was a splice, and not just a hybrid? He pulled her top lip up to look at her teeth. No, she was no vampire. But her mate was… Could it be?

The idea in his head made him giddy. Like a surprise present. Was she pregnant?

He grabbed her arm and shook her. No response. He pulled her shirt up to just under her breasts and looked at her stomach. She was covered in bruises and wounds from her beating, but not one blow had obviously landed lower than her ribs. He laid his palm against her flesh, just under her navel. An electric shock shot into his hand, and he jumped, pulling back. Red currents snaked over Forest's skin where he'd touched her. He poked at the marks with his index finger and received a stronger sting than before. The electric, protective barrier was only on her stomach.

He laughed and sat back, amused and amazed. Oh, she was pregnant all right. Pregnant by a vampire mage, who now was rumored to look like a god of lightning. The odd, gentle part of him felt soft and warm toward the unborn child. They were his kin. Family. But that was quickly replaced by wrath. His hate for Forest reared up and choked him. So jealous of the measure of happiness she'd been able to have. She had love, home, position, the affection of their father, and now she had a child of her own.

Well, she had too much. It wasn't good for her to have so much. She was spoiled.

He looked at her stomach closely, his eyes sliding out of focus. A child of three races. Not so different from himself. He'd brought many things with him when he'd come back to Regia. Magical objects he might need to progress his plans. He never would have thought what he would need the most would be in the bowels of the *Rune-dy*. Well, he'd get what he needed, and he knew who would give it to him.

Chapter Four

Reports of the strike were pouring into the *Rune-dy*. The usual cold composure of the priests was only slightly ruffled around the edges. Camber kept coming in and out, interrupting them with new developments, mostly in the form of scrolls. The stiff rules and formality was disturbed as Camber was forced to bring a few people that had no right to be there into the *Rune-dy's* headquarters. But they were admitted to share their eyewitness accounts of what they had experienced in the strike.

Rahaxeris tried to find his footing as the others looked to him to lead. He desperately wanted to shout at the other priests to have their own think tank without him for a while, so he could check on Forest.

As he read the reports, he began glancing up often at Menjel. Menjel read the reports after he did but held his feelings—if he had any—in better control than Rahaxeris was able. They were not on the same page. As far as Rahaxeris could tell, Menjel wasn't bothered in the slightest by what Copernicus had done.

Why didn't he care? Copernicus was more his creation than Rahaxeris'. Splicing all the races together in one was Menjel's idea during the course of the experiment. The same experiment that found Rahaxeris in love with Liasia and resulted in Forest being born.

The memory of Copernicus' creation rushed on him with shame. He wasn't going to use his own blood, never had that crossed his mind. But Menjel was angry at him about Forest at the time. He'd been looking through his scope at the petri-dish filled with everything Copernicus was going to be, when Menjel came up beside him, grabbed his hand, and pricked his finger. The drop of blood fell into the dish. Cursing Menjel, Rahaxeris grabbed the dish, about to dash it to the floor when Menjel restrained his hand.

"No. Leave it. You've been so keen to throw your DNA into the work before. Let's see what it does this time."

Rahaxeris obeyed. Menjel was the high priest.

He watched Copernicus grow in a tube, never expecting him to survive, *hoping* he wouldn't. Rahaxeris had breathed a sigh of relief when Copernicus began to deteriorate; the races were not gelling together. He'd expected Copernicus to die quickly, but again, Menjel stepped in. Being the superior scientist and much more ruthless, Menjel had nursed Copernicus along with Malachi Serum; a brutal chemical compound that worked as an adjuvant, effectively binding the races together and poisoning Copernicus at the same time.

Copernicus grew up fast, excessively violent, and totally insane. Menjel wanted him as a weapon, but he was too volatile, often crashing into fits of tears and deep depressions. One second he was a skilled killer, the next he wanted to cuddle the target. He killed ruthlessly but then fell into heartbreaking remorse for the life he'd taken.

As far as his body was concerned, he was a success. All the races together inside one person, but his psyche was broken, weak, and shaky. Rahaxeris had wanted to kill him to put him out of his misery, but Menjel refused his requests.

Copernicus grew to adulthood faster than anyone could have anticipated. He was dangerous. Uncontrollable. He escaped from the *Rune-dy* and ran amuck across Regia, leaving behind a trail of blood and a notorious name. Rahaxeris was only half as powerful then and doubted his own ability to take Copernicus down. In a moment of naked desperation, he had sought the assistance of a wizard. *Take care of it* were the only instructions Rahaxeris gave Maxcarion, and that became a deep regret of his as well.

Maxcarion hadn't killed Copernicus. Instead, he sent him off world and wouldn't tell Rahaxeris where. Rahaxeris would have pursued the matter, but again, Menjel blocked him. To his shame, he didn't buck Menjel because he felt like his hands were tied because of his attempts to climb the ladder to high priest, to change things…for his baby girl.

Rahaxeris refocused his eyes on the report in front of him, reading about how nothing was left of the Fair. His mind twisted around trying to figure out what Copernicus' main goal was in the whole strike. Why would the Fair be hit harder than anywhere else? Cold dread filled him.

The other priests had been talking around the table; he hadn't been listening to them. Their chatter was background noise, alerting him only when they all fell silent at once. Rahaxeris looked up. They were all staring at him. Camber was back, a stranger at his side.

Rahaxeris' chair legs scraped the floor loudly as he got up. He moved to the stranger, snatched the letter from his hands, and unfolded it. A lock of bronze hair fell from the parchment into his hand. The shade of bronze was familiar, too familiar. He read the few words of the letter, then pierced the stranger with his eyes, his heart icing over.

Menjel came up behind him and grabbed the letter, reading it himself. He gave Rahaxeris an odd, flat look. "Go. I'll handle everything else."

It was the wrong thing to do. He knew it clearly. Copernicus had Forest. She might already be dead. The thought made his spirit cry out. No, she couldn't be dead. Surely if she were dead, he'd know, because Syrus would know. He couldn't see Syrus sitting still in his grief, no, not an anger ball like Syrus. If Forest was already dead, Regia as a whole would know it.

Going to Copernicus was the wrong thing to do. But what choice did he have? The weight of being a parent, the instinct that existed without logic, and the concrete fact that he would trade his life for hers without looking back, moved him to nod his head.

"Don't follow," Rahaxeris ordered the other priests.

The silent stranger smiled, flashing Forest's ring on his finger, and opened a portal, taking Rahaxeris with him.

The priests looked apprehensively at Menjel and all began demanding what was going on.

"Calm down. Copernicus has kidnapped Forest and is trying to ransom her. In case any of you are unaware, our high priest, powerful as he may be, is terribly weak when it comes to his child. I don't think we can expect him to return. So, now, again, as it has been before, I am now high priest."

"You can't just do that," Cassian piped up. "It goes against our regulations. Rahaxeris usually leaves you in charge when he is gone, but you can't just take over without due process."

Menjel curled his lip at Cassian. "You're right." His voice was colder than usual. "That's all I meant. I'm in charge for now. Until Rahaxeris comes back." He turned his attention to Camber. "Have anything else to deliver?"

"No, sir."

"Then get out."

"Yes, sir." Camber left quickly.

Camber was gone only a few moments before he was back, another stranger hanging behind him. "An urgent message for you, sir," he said to Menjel.

Menjel strode up to the messenger. He held no message. His face was shadowed in a hood.

"I come from Copernicus. I must speak to Menjel in private."

The priests watched in shock as Menjel admitted the man and led him out of their main room.

"Something stinks here," Hezeron said quietly.

Everyone nodded in agreement.

****

Rahaxeris landed on his feet and straightened up, squinting. The sunlight bounced off the surface of the rose-colored water and into his eyes. The deck of the ship rocked under his feet. He wondered where Copernicus could have found this vessel. Travel or trade on the water had not been a common Regian practice for hundreds of years. His choice to hide on the water was a shrewd move. Rahaxeris had to give him that. He glared at the man next to him.

"Who are you?" he demanded of the messenger.

The man shifted out of the elf façade. Rahaxeris inhaled sharply as his memories jolted.

"Copernicus."

The man laughed lightly and shook his head. "No. I'm not. Spitting image, I know. My name is Shreve."

Rahaxeris examined him closely. "*What* are you?"

49

Shreve didn't get the chance to answer. The door in the deck floor opened, and the real Copernicus emerged. He came up behind Shreve, leaned down, and whispered something in his ear. Shreve gave Copernicus a pained look but left and went down the stairs into the belly of the ship, leaving Rahaxeris and Copernicus alone. The next second, another portal opened on the deck, and a hooded figure came through it. His face was shadowed, and he carried a glass vial of some cloudy grey liquid.

"Is that it?" Copernicus asked him.

The hooded figure nodded and went below deck, and they were alone again.

For a moment, they just stared at one another. Copernicus' face flushed, and his hands shook.

"It's been so long, Father."

"Don't call me that."

Copernicus looked as though he might cry. "Why? You are my father."

"In a way, I suppose. Where is Forest?"

Copernicus smiled. "Not yet. You'll see her soon. She's here. Our family is all together. You, me, Shreve, Forest, and the baby."

"Baby?" A cold wave of terror washed over Rahaxeris.

"Oh, you didn't know? Forest is pregnant. Congratulations, Grandpa."

Rahaxeris tried to appear unaffected by this news. He hoped, with his whole being, it was a lie.

"Have you hurt her?"

"Yes, I must say that I have. In fact, I think I may have gone too far. She won't wake." Copernicus' emotional side came out, and he wiped at a tear in the corner of his eye. "I'm a little too passionate about my sister. There's no knowing what I might do to her. I love her...and I hate her... almost more than I hate you."

"Please," Rahaxeris whispered.

"Please what?"

"She's my child."

"And what am I? You never explained anything to me."

"An experiment. You should have been destroyed."

He growled and slapped Rahaxeris across the face.

Rahaxeris staggered but didn't move to strike back. He smoothed the front of his robe. "What do you want? How do I get you to let Forest go?"

"Why do you care so much about her?!" he shouted. "Why does she have your love, and all I have is your contempt?"

"What do you want from me?" Rahaxeris asked again.

"Everything!" he roared. Then, he took a deep breath and schooled his face and voice. "You will submit to my control. You are going to stand behind me in an unwavering show of support of my claim to the throne. Regia fears you. I will use that. No one will dare even think about standing against me with you at my side."

"That's all? I support you, and you'll let Forest go?"

"That's all."

"Well, I'm here. I agree. So let her go."

Copernicus smiled broadly. "I will. Come... Come see her."

Rahaxeris followed Copernicus through the door in the deck down a short flight of stairs. There was a hallway with four doors; three were shut, one stood slightly ajar. Copernicus stood aside and gestured for Rahaxeris to enter the room ahead of him. Desperate to see what had befallen Forest, Rahaxeris ignored his better judgment and went through the door.

She was laid out on the floor, her skin mottled in bruises. Cuts covered her face and arms. The whole room was splattered with blood, even the ceiling. Panicked, he rushed to her, only to be jerked backward by the throat. Rahaxeris gagged against the metal cuff now locked around his neck.

"Shhh...Shhh... Hold still, it won't hurt so much if you hold still," Copernicus crooned in his ear. "Don't fight it."

A bright flash of heat surged up his neck. The heat pushed up into the top of his head before sliding back down through his whole body. All of his power drained away, not just his magic, but everything down to his ability to hold himself upright.

Rahaxeris crashed to the floor, weak like a dying old man. His power along with his rage was there inside him, but he couldn't access them, as though they were shut inside a vault. He had rage, but rage took energy to manifest, and he had no energy at all. The cuff absorbed it all.

Copernicus looked down at him, a satisfied smile on his broad face. "Surprised, aren't you? How does it feel to have everything taken away? I brought that little trinket back with me from the wizards. Now you're mine, and you can do nothing to double cross me, as I know you would have."

Copernicus reached down and lifted Rahaxeris under the arms. He maneuvered him into a sitting position against the wall, where he could see Forest. Copernicus sat down cross-legged next to him. He smiled as he looked at her.

"She's so beautiful. You must be proud of her, all she's accomplished."

"Yes," Rahaxeris said faintly. He saw no point in lying now.

"I'm not going to let her go. You know that, don't you?"

"I knew it before I came."

"Then why did you come?" Copernicus demanded.

"I had to try. Please don't hurt her anymore. I can hear her heart. You put her on a dangerous edge. She still might not make it if you don't do something to heal her... Let me."

"No. I'm not taking that off your neck. Not ever."

"But she's—"

"She needs something all right," Copernicus cut him off. "It's too bad about the child."

"What do you mean?"

Copernicus put his hands behind his head and leaned back against the wall, lazily. "I learned a lot about myself when Maxcarion sent me to the wizards. Wizards have a great capacity for cruelty. And they are more skilled at science than the *Rune-dy*. Their skill set is rather different, I'll admit. But they are incapable of letting something they do not understand lay still. They cannot leave a puzzle alone. I was one such puzzle when I got there. They continued the work you began, adding to the races already meshed together inside me. I can say with pride, I am unique."

Rahaxeris said nothing.

Copernicus sighed and continued. "They deconstructed me... Come to find out, there was a key element inside me I couldn't live without. Malachi Serum. That's what Forest needs now."

Rahaxeris blanched. "No!"

"Come now, think about it." Copernicus got to his feet. "She has a child of three races in her belly. The baby needs the serum to survive. Shreve, bring me that vial!" he yelled toward the door.

Shreve came in holding the accursed grey liquid and a syringe. Rahaxeris eyed it. That syringe came from the *Rune-dy*. It was Menjel's favorite style to work with. Oh, if he ever got out of this, he'd kill Menjel slowly on his own operating table for this.

"What's going on?" Shreve asked, looking suspiciously at Copernicus as he handed him the vial and syringe.

"Watch and learn," Copernicus said to Shreve.

"Don't do this! Please! You'll kill her!" Rahaxeris begged.

Copernicus drew the liquid into the syringe. "I'm trying to help the baby. It's too mixed, like me. I want it to live...and Forest is strong. It will probably do her good as well, seeing as she's a hybrid."

He moved toward her and knelt down, the needle catching the light.

"Stop! She doesn't need it because she is natural! She was born. Her baby doesn't need it because it is natural! *You* needed it to survive because you were grown in a tube."

Copernicus' face whipped to Rahaxeris, a crazed fury in his eyes. "Does that mean I don't have a soul?!"

"I don't know!"

"Forget to add that to my ingredient list? One soul."

He turned back to Forest and plunged the needle into her arm.

"No!" Rahaxeris clawed at the metal around his neck. "Stop! You're killing her!"

Chapter Five

Syrus left Ithiel and the masters with orders to stay in the Onyx Castle and assist Zeren. He took Merhl and five other ogres with him back to where he'd found Forest's sword on the ground. He stood back as the ogres combed the area, trying to catch the signature of a portal that might have been opened there by Forest's kidnapper.

He stretched his magic out through the area, trying to glean anything he could.

"My lord, Syrus," Merhl broke through his focus. "I found something. Not much. Nothing we can catch and re-open, I'm afraid. But I found the trace only because it has my signature on it."

"What?"

"The portal was created by Forest's own ring. I'm sorry. There is nothing else here."

Syrus turned away from Merhl and exhaled, breaking down into shards inside. The hope he'd been holding close to his chest turned to dust. What did he do now? He looked down at Forest's sword in his hand and thought again of where he'd found it, hidden on the ground. It had to have been Redge. It had to have been. Was Redge with her now? Was he with the enemy? How could he find him?

"What can I do?" Merhl asked desperately. "Let me help, please."

"Merhl, go to the *Rune-dy* and bring Rahaxeris back here."

"Yes, sir. Of course."

"And open a portal for me back to Halussis."

"Back to the Onyx Castle, sir?" Merhl asked.

"No." Syrus had a sudden premonition about where he might find Redge. "Open a portal to the rural outskirts of the city."

Merhl nodded quickly and struck the air with the flat of his hand. Syrus strapped Forest's sword around his waist and moved toward the portal when he abruptly fell onto his knees. The sound of Forest's heartbeat, coupled with the racing pulse of the baby thundered through him. Forest's steady rhythm skipped, spluttered, and screamed. His lungs refused to fill, his heart turned to stone. She was dying. Forest was dying.

He got back to his feet and ran into the black portal. Time set its hideous face against him. He didn't know how much longer she had.

Syrus only took a second to gain his bearings when his feet hit the ground. The area was devoid of life except for the plants. He ran forward, unable to feel the ground under his feet. His heartbeat mixed in his ears along with Forest's and the baby's. His body moved faster and faster as his soul clung to the edge of a thin blade. Loss and pain ran like the devil behind him, just on his heels. He hacked at tree limbs and hanging vines as they grabbed at him, trying to slow him down.

"Redge!" he shouted. "Are you here?!"

A ruin of a house loomed ahead of him. The look of it struck a chord with his memory.

"Redge!" he shouted again.

For one second, the space of time between one heartbeat and the next, Syrus didn't breathe.

Redge appeared in the doorway. "Syrus, what are you—"

"Where is she?"

Redge opened his mouth and then shut it, shaking his head. "I can't tell you."

Syrus roared and ran at his oldest friend, lifting him off his feet, pushing him back into the house until his back crashed against the crumbling stone wall.

"Where is she? Where is she?" Syrus shouted in Redge's face. "Tell me, damn you! She's dying! I have to save her!"

Redge pushed back at Syrus. "I *can't* tell you! Don't you think I would if I could? I'm a slave."

Lightning cracked and snaked up Syrus' arms. Redge's eyes went wide one second before Syrus slammed his fist into his face. Redge fell to the ground, but Syrus lifted him up again. Redge swung back in defense, his knuckles cracking into Syrus' jaw. Redge may as well have punched the wall for all the effect it had.

"She's dying! Right now!"

"He *made* me take her. I had no choice. He made me kidnap her, he made me beat her…" The words slipped out.

The fire in Syrus' eyes flashed into an inferno. *"You beat her?!"*

"I'm sorry, Syrus. You have no idea how damn sorry!"

Nonsensical and unfair as it might have been, everything Syrus was feeling, he transferred to Redge. He pulled Forest's sword from its scabbard.

Redge's eyes bugged. "Shit!" He darted away, grabbing his own sword, and held it up in a block.

The obsidian glass blade sliced through Redge's sword, breaking it in two. He dropped the now pointless hilt and exhaled, waiting for his best friend to kill him. Redge's face and voice went calm and serious as Syrus thrust the blade beneath his chin.

"Do it," he said quietly. "Kill me. At least then I can't hurt anyone else."

The fire in Syrus' eyes stilled. He blinked.

"Do it," he said again. "I can't live as a slave anymore. As my friend, it would be a kindness to me."

Syrus' lip curled, and he pulled the sword back from his neck and sheathed it. He turned his back on Redge and walked away. He stopped in the doorway and looked over his shoulder. "We're not friends anymore."

Then Syrus was gone.

****

Copernicus left Rahaxeris against the wall in Forest's room. The ship bobbed on the waves as the night darkened the space. Unable to do anything else, Rahaxeris crawled on the floor toward Forest. He reached her, exhausted from the effort and placed his hand on her arm over the injection site. His fingers shook against her skin as he attempted to use his power to pull the poison back out of her. Nothing happened. He listened to her heartbeat. Her veins moved the serum through her whole body. She didn't have much time left. A few hours. She probably wouldn't last the night.

If only he could remove the collar around his neck, he could save her life. His long fingers picked slowly at the hinge and the clasp. He worked at the pin in the hinge with his feeble, almost useless fingers. He was getting nowhere with it, but it was the only thing he could do, so he kept at it. He wouldn't give up, so long as she still lived, he would try whatever he could.

A very dim light fell across him on the floor as the door creaked open. Rahaxeris turned and looked at the silhouette standing on the threshold. The figure hesitated a moment and then stepped into the room and shut the door behind him.

Shreve moved to Rahaxeris and knelt down next to him. He looked intently at Forest. "She's dying, isn't she?" he asked quietly.

"Yes," Rahaxeris whispered.

Shreve stared at her for a moment, a blank look on his face. He turned his full attention on to Rahaxeris. "Look at me closely, please."

Rahaxeris looked.

"What am I?" Shreve asked.

Rahaxeris felt his surprise weakly. He reached out and took a hold of Shreve's wrist, pressing down on his pulse. After a moment of analyzing, he let go.

"Why do you call Copernicus father?" Rahaxeris asked.

"It's what I've been led to believe my whole life. That he is my father. And yet I've always doubted it. It's not the truth, is it? He's not really my father, is he?"

"No, he's not your father. He's your original. You're a clone, Shreve."

Shreve sat down on the floor and laced his fingers together, looking intently at his own hands. "You didn't make me?"

"No, I didn't. The wizards must have."

"I'm not really sure about all of this. Copernicus's whole plan, I mean. I spent my childhood with the wizards. I don't think Copernicus can hold them back the way he thinks he can if he takes the throne. What do you think?"

"Are the wizards really coming to take over Regia?" Rahaxeris asked.

"Yes. Regia and many other worlds as well."

"Nothing Copernicus could do, king or not, will stop them."

"Could you stop them? Could the *Rune-dy*?"

"I don't know. But I will take your word that they truly are coming," Rahaxeris said. "I will think on it."

Shreve sighed and turned his attention back to Forest. "What's it worth to you, if I let you save her life?"

"Everything."

"I've watched her for a while now. Copernicus had me follow her for a long time. She's a good person and she's a good leader… In some twisted way, she is my sister. I don't want her to die."

Rahaxeris narrowed his eyes at Shreve. "You're not like your original. Same face, same DNA, different mind."

Shreve nodded. "The things he does… In almost every circumstance… He chooses differently than I would."

"If you take this collar off me for just a moment, I could reverse the poison in Forest's blood. You have my word I will do nothing else. Just please, let me save my daughter and her child."

Shreve's jaw tightened, and he reached for the clasp on the collar.

Chapter Six

Journey experienced a naked, desperate, raging hope and equal parts crippling fear. She hid in the shadows and watched. All these years apart, Journey held Redge frozen inside her heart. His face, trapped in youth, her love for him unmoving, silent, and waiting. She didn't know what this moment would do to her, but she'd had her doubts that what she had felt long ago, what she remembered feeling, would prove to be no more than a phantom now. As her eyes drank the image of him, here, alive, in front of her, it was the doubt that became the phantom. The ice she'd encased him in melted away, and her heart shocked to life in a burst of bright electric current.

Tears fell silently as she continued to hold still. Was she really still? She was burning, reaching, pulsing. Hungry life raced through her body, just under the skin. She clamped her hands over her mouth to keep from crying out. She wanted to run to him and dive into his arms; it was killing her to hold still.

Did he ever think of her, dream of her? Was it possible? Did she dare recognize the hope that he still loved her? Had he ever really loved her? Did she still have a place in his heart? She was the one who had run away after all, realizing her mistake one moment after it was too late to turn around.

She'd told herself the reason she came back after all these years was to warn him his world was about to be invaded by the wizards. That was the solid thought in her mind, and it was the incentive that forced her to jump over the edge. Journey had always wanted to come back to him but always felt that desire was foolish and selfish—not to mention illegal.

She'd been plagued for so long, not having the answers of what had really happened that night. The night she ran away. She realized that she didn't understand what she saw and cursed herself for not allowing him to explain. Even now, the bloody memory of Redge taking a life right in front of her sent a roll of cold fear down her spine. She shook it off.

He'd changed. Matured into a man. His shoulders were broader than she remembered, his walk steady, purposeful. She looked intently at his hands. They were rough, scarred, and moved with determination. He was an impressive man. His face, now well past the youth she knew, was beyond her many fantasies of what he might look like now. When he turned her way and she got a clear, straight-on view of him, her mouth fell open. *Oh, my*, was all her brain could articulate at first.

She admired him slowly and meticulously, taking in every detail of his appearance and demeanor. He paced back and forth through the trees, stress and sorrow filling the air around him. His roughly beautiful face was pulled into a hard frown. She was too far away to read his heart, but even if she had been standing in front of him, she would have been too scared. As a Storyteller, she could reach inside him and answer every question she had. But would the answers crush her? She'd already risked so much, and gaining the knowledge of what was in his heart was the biggest risk of all.

He went back inside the crumbling structure and started to organize and shift the skeletons of furniture around. She could see him though the holes in the walls and the open windows and door. He cleaned the space as if trying to make it livable. Why had he banished himself to this graveyard of memories?

There was no noise, no one else around for miles. They were alone together, and yet, still apart.

Journey waited until the dark fell and shrouded the trees, until the shadows reached, expanded, and came together in full night. She moved without sound to the doorway of the ruin and paused. He was asleep on the bare, weathered frame of a bed. She shivered in response to his close proximity. It was unlike any shiver she'd ever experienced. It lingered and buzzed almost painfully.

I love you, she thought. *I never stopped.*

The urge to look inside him gnawed with sharp teeth. She could know it all right now. She could read his heart while he slept. And if she couldn't find any remains of herself there, she could leave without him ever knowing she'd been there at all. She could deliver the message of the wizards' approaching danger another way.

Read him. Journey trembled against the instinct. Not yet. It was still just a fantasy. One she wasn't ready to let go of.

She listened to his breathing, watching his chest rise and fall. His eyes moved behind his eyelids, and his hands flexed once. She held her breath then relaxed; he was dreaming.

Journey sat down on the dirt floor. She wanted to touch him so badly. Just to rest her hand on his, but she didn't dare. The location, this house, this man, turned a key in her mind and let loose one of her most precious memories. She closed her eyes and watched.

Journey had just told her first story in Regia and was elated and exhausted. She'd been well trained before she decided to travel the channels, but this was her first real story, pulled from real people, who sat still, anxious for the experience. She felt good in her performance. Confident she'd done a good job. Everyone left with a smile on his or her face.

As the crowd moved away from her, she turned and noticed she was being watched. The young man leaned casually against a tree, his arms crossed over his chest. He stared unabashedly at her. He was about the same age as she, a youth on the edge of adulthood. She faced him fully and returned his gaze, a pull hooking her right through the stomach. His eyes were deep dark water, a current of green under the midnight blue.

What did he want? A story? If so, why hadn't he joined the crowd? Maybe it was the first time he'd seen a Storyteller, and he didn't know how to participate. Well, she should tell him. He might need the healing a story could bring. She took a step toward him, intending to explain her abilities, when he straightened and walked away.

He came to the place she told stories every day, but he never joined the crowd. He simply watched. At first, she thought he was watching the story, but she quickly realized he was only there to watch her. She pulled out all the stops as she worked, showing off for him. Her whole body seemed to light up under his gaze. He never spoke to her. Every time she tried to approach him, he would turn away and leave. She began to think of how she might trap him, just to get a few words out of him, or get close enough to read him.

He continued to show up every day for two weeks, but then one day he wasn't there. His absence flustered her. She felt the emptiness of the space he usually filled acutely, painfully. Where was he? Why hadn't he come? Was he all right? Had he simply just lost interest? Journey told her stories, but her mind wandered as she worked.

When the crowds left that day, Journey walked in the direction he always went when he was finished watching her. She didn't know if she even had a chance of finding him; he might have been on the other side of Regia for all she knew. She couldn't even ask anybody if they might know where he was because she didn't know his name. But she continued to move forward, still flustered and compelled.

She came to an area that was lush and full of life. The sun felt warmer than usual as it filtered through the trees. It heated her skin and reached all the way down to her bones. She grew warmer and warmer as she thought about him and the way he always looked at her. Journey began to walk faster, some primal instinct told her he was close by.

She turned toward the sound of water running and came upon a river. There he was, standing on the opposite bank, facing her.

"I knew you'd come," he said.

"How did you know?"

"Because I wanted it. I wanted you to come to me so badly I was sure you would feel it... And I was right."

He was so cocky she had to make an attempt not to be annoyed. After all, she was there with no reason for being there except to find him. His gaze hooked her straight through the core again, and the magnetism that pulled on her would have had her crashing into him had it not been for the water rushing between them.

"My name's Journey. What's yours?"

"Redge. And I already knew your name. I've known it since the first day I saw you. I asked around."

Her gaze pulled away from his, moving down to his chest. He quickly placed his hand like a barrier over his heart.

"No." His voice was forceful. "Don't read me."

She looked back into his eyes, confused. No one had ever tried to block her. "Why not? Why do you only watch? Why don't you join the group?"

The heat of his gaze grew more intense, and a confident smile pulled at the side of his mouth. "Maybe I want to tell you a story. I'll show you what's in my heart, if you show me what's in yours."

"That's not how it works. I'm a healer. I can help rid you of the things that weigh you down. I do good for others. You don't have to fear it. I read people every day. It's not personal."

He raised one eyebrow and took a step forward, into the water. "Not personal? You're totally wrong about that."

The pull in her stomach gave a little tug, and she took a step into the river as well, the water pleasantly cool. What was she doing?

"If you read me, it would be personal, Journey. Too personal."

He took another step forward, the water up to his knees. She took another step as well. The hem of her dress pulled and moved with the current.

They came together in the center of the river, the water rushing around their waists. He reached out and took both of her hands.

"Why do you watch me every day?" she asked.

"You know why."

Journey swallowed. "What is this?"

"A beginning."

Journey looked back at his chest.

"Don't!" he said roughly.

"Sorry, it's a natural thing for me to do. And since you've told me not to, I want to more than ever."

"How much control do you have over the stories you tell?"

"Total control."

"Let go of that control and see what happens…"

He kissed her then, his mouth greedy with the passion of youth.

The memory assailed her system and spun her head. Her body remembered so acutely. She opened her eyes and looked at him again. Time had altered him, just as it had her. They were strangers. But just being next to him, the chemical reaction that had always lived and raged between them resurrected, undamaged by time. Her breath exhaled on a shudder as she mourned the years they had not been together.

She sat next to him for a while. As he slept, she remembered so much more.

Redge became restless, his dreams obviously disturbed him. She wanted to help, it was in her nature, but again she held back. When they were young, he'd never wanted her to read him without his permission. So she didn't read him now. He mumbled in his sleep. A solitary tear pushed out through his closed eyelids and ran down. She left him then. She couldn't be still next to him while he suffered like that.

Journey glanced at him over her shoulder as she left the ruin. She found another ruin close by and decided to make it her temporary dwelling. She sank down in a corner, letting her head rest against the hard stone wall. Redge called out in his sleep, a strangled cry of pain and frustration. The sound stabbed her through the soul. She put her hands over her mouth and wept.

Journey dozed a little as the sun rose in the sky. She heard him stirring, listened to his movements. She got up quietly, her back stiff, and looked toward his ruin from the window of hers. It looked as though he was continuing the work of cleaning and sorting through the remains of the house. He mumbled to himself. She couldn't understand the actual words he spoke aloud, but the resonance of his voice told of regret and anger, sometimes shifting into a tone of determination.

He came out through the doorway carrying an armful of rocks. She moved to the side where he couldn't see her. Carefully, she peeked through the window, allowing only the smallest, amount of her face necessary to see, past the rough frame. Redge worked through the morning in solitude. No one came into the area. She wondered again why he was here. There seemed to be no point.

He stopped what he was doing and looked up at the sky. Her heart stilled as she watched him find a scrap of parchment and a pen. He wrote only a few words, but he spoke as he marked them.

"Journey, I love you. Help me."

Then he lit the scrap on fire. He held it as it quickly burned to nothing, a small tendril of smoke drifting upward. He watched the smoke for a moment, then he looked down and sighed, shaking his head. As the smoke dissipated into nothing, his voice whispered the same words she just heard him say in her mind. *Journey, I love you. Help me.*

She bit down on her lip to keep from crying out. How could it be? All these years she'd wanted to believe the messages were from him, but she always doubted it was really true. He'd never missed a single day. Did he know she heard him?

****

Never had Syrus been in such darkness. He thought about the baby he would never meet. The child of their love. Their souls intertwined in a completely new person. The end was upon him. He felt Forest's life slipping away like sand blown by the wind. It was too late. There was nothing he could do. Nothing but tell her goodbye. He closed his eyes, both his hands over his heart, and sent her his farewell. *I love you…I love you…You will take my soul away with you and leave me hollow…Forever.*

Chapter Seven

The Malachi Serum flowing through Forest's veins entered the baby's bloodstream, adhering to the tiny heart, causing a spark of red electricity to flash with each little beat, twisting the little organ with irreparable damage.

Rahaxeris' hand shook violently as he gripped Forest's arm over the injection site. His red eyes clamped shut with pain and effort as he pulled the poison back from her extremities, back down to her arm, where it wept out slowly and absorbed into him.

Shreve waited nervously, the magical cuff in his hands, ready to put it back on Rahaxeris. "Is it done?" His voice was desperate.

"Yes," Rahaxeris whispered, accepting the cuff back around his neck.

Damage had been done to Forest that Rahaxeris could do nothing about, but she would live, at least for now. He'd bought her a little more time. To recover fully, Forest needed Syrus. His healing abilities had grown to a level Rahaxeris marveled over. And if the child was to survive at all, it would be Syrus who could save its life.

Weakness rushed through Rahaxeris again as the clasp locked down. The serum he'd taken into himself was making him sick, but he could take a lot more before it did much of anything. A few hours, and he wouldn't feel its effects at all.

"I have to go now." Shreve made to leave the room.

"Thank you." Rahaxeris sighed. "I'll never forget this kindness."

Shreve nodded once and shut the door behind him.

Forest's heart began to beat strong again, her breathing sped up, and then she gasped, waking in the dark. He reached and placed his sharp hand gently on her forearm.

"It's all right, Forest. I'm here."

A small sob rose up her throat. "Father?"

"Yes."

She groaned. "What's wrong with me? I've never felt anything like this."

"You were poisoned while in a death sleep. And perhaps *some* of what you're feeling is nothing more than the result of the life growing inside you."

She gripped his hand tightly with hers. "How do you know? Can you sense it?" she demanded urgently.

"I was told before I ever had the chance. Copernicus knows."

"No," she rasped. "I wanted to keep it a secret."

"Well, it's not, so we have to deal with him knowing."

"You sound strange. I can't really see you. Why haven't you just kicked his ass yet and taken me out of here?"

"He used you to bait me. For the moment, I can do nothing. He has hobbled me. So we have to use our heads to get out of this. But as I'm sure you've noticed, Copernicus is insane, as soft and weak as he is cruel and deadly. Every encounter you have with him…"

"I must invoke his pity," she said.

Rahaxeris smiled in the dark. "Yes, exactly."

She groaned again, flexing her hands over her stomach. "Oh no…" she breathed.

70

"What is it?"

"You said I was poisoned... The baby?"

He must not scare her with his own fears. "I pulled the poison from you before it could kill you."

"But what has it done to my baby?" Her voice rose.

"Shhh... Don't fear. If the poison reached the baby, once we get you out, Syrus can heal you, both of you. Have no doubt of that. That's his child. It will respond and thrive under its father's power."

Forest let out a ragged breath, calming down slightly. "So how do we get out?"

"That will depend on what Copernicus does next. But you are alive only because of Shreve."

"What?"

"He might be false, time will tell. But he appears to be our ally. If Copernicus separates us—as I fear he might—if you can, stay close to Shreve."

They were quiet for a while as the dawn threatened, its faint light easing down through the skylight over Forest. The ship rocked them lazily. She moved her hands back and forth slowly over her abdomen. The thump of footfalls on the deck overhead alerted them both. Forest looked at Rahaxeris.

"What should I do?" she whispered.

"Copernicus wasn't able to wake you when I got here—you were in a death sleep. I suggest you play dead."

****

Thump... thump... thump...thump

Syrus' eyes shot open as Forest's dying heartbeat rallied and thundered with life. He could scarcely breathe, dazed with gratitude. There weren't words strong enough for what he felt. She sent his heart a rushing wave of love straight from hers. She was alive. He had another chance to save his family. He took up her sword and jumped to his feet.

The pale sunlight shot into his eyes as he looked up into the morning sky. He swore to himself he would have her back before the sun dawned another day. But what to do next? Why wasn't Rahaxeris helping him get Forest back? Why hadn't Merhl delivered the *Rune-dy* as he'd ordered? He needed Rahaxeris' help.

He returned to the house and rummaged around in Forest's jewelry until he found an extra End of the Bridge. Ogres could open portals, *Rune-dy* could open portals, but he was stuck with his feet without the little trinket.

Syrus crushed the little silvery ball in his hand and opened a portal to Kyhael. He was alarmed as the portal dumped him in the antechamber of the *Rune-dy*. What had happened to their security measures? How could his portal put him right inside their headquarters?

Instinct sparked, and Syrus moved silently to the circle of light on the wall, sword in hand. Something was very wrong. Danger filled this place like a pungent fog.

He put his hand over the light beam and waited for it to expand large enough to let him through. The main room was devoid of life but full of death. The priests lay strewn on the floor, their blood still warm, running over the stone. He hesitated. Whoever could kill the *Rune-dy* was no one he wanted to tangle with. His eyes took in the violent scene and he counted the bodies. Four. Rahaxeris wasn't among the dead, at least not in this room, neither was the twist Menjel.

Low voices carried into the room from down the hall. Syrus didn't move or breathe.

"You've proven your loyalty, Menjel. Killing them was easier than I thought it would be."

"Well, in their defense, they were caught off guard," Menjel said. "So what do you plan to do next?"

"I'm going to take my throne."

"How are you going to do that, Copernicus?" Menjel asked.

"Don't worry about it. Once it becomes public knowledge that I have Rahaxeris in submission…and your open support as well, the fear will spread like a plague."

"Did you kill Forest?"

Syrus clenched his teeth. There was a short silence from the other room.

"She's not your concern," Copernicus snapped finally.

"You're right. And I don't care what happens to her, but the people… You don't want her as a martyr. She has the love of many, since she rose to power. The people learning you killed her could easily cause an uprising against your new claim to the throne."

"I didn't kill my sister! She is safe and hidden. In time, she will stand with me as well as Rahaxeris. Her child will call me father, and Forest will sit on the throne next to me."

Menjel laughed. "How deliciously incestuous of you, Copernicus. So, I assume you intend to kill Syrus then?"

"When the time is right."

"Why not try your luck right now?" Syrus growled as he came into the room.

Before Menjel could do anything other than jump in alarm, Syrus hit him with a band of lightning that snaked around him like a rope. He

73

fell to the floor, his arms and legs bound together. Copernicus stood slowly, facing Syrus down.

Syrus held the hilt of Forest's sword with both hands, the blade at the ready in front of him. Never had he been so thirsty for another's death. This thirst would not slacken until it was completely satisfied.

"The reports were true, mage. You *do* look like a god of lightning," Copernicus said as he drew his own sword. "Nice blade, never seen one like it. I'll enjoy claiming it once you're dead, just as I'll claim everything else that is yours. Your mate, your child, and what could have been your throne."

Syrus didn't care for trash talk at this moment. He attacked. Copernicus stepped back, trying to deflect Syrus' strikes. His blade blocked two hits before it shattered against the black glass. Copernicus ducked as the sword sliced through the space his head had just occupied. He half shifted into beast form when the glass blade sliced across his chest sideways. Copernicus cried out, grabbing at his torn flesh, but he had no time. Syrus sliced him again down the side of his neck, a move meant to cut off his head, but he fell to the side and onto the floor.

His beast arm grabbed Syrus by the foot. Syrus brought the sword down, stabbing straight through Copernicus' forearm.

Syrus pulled the sword up and swung it high before bringing it down again in a strike that should have ended Copernicus. Instead, the end of the blade stabbed into a portal. Copernicus had fled for his life. The portal closed in the blink of an eye, before Syrus could pursue him through it.

Syrus swore a string of curses and fell on his knees. He looked over at Menjel, still tied up on the floor, convulsing as the lightning electrocuted him repeatedly. He sheathed the sword and got back to his feet. Syrus pulled the power back to himself and hauled Menjel up by the front of his robes.

"If there is anything you can do, or any information you can give that will help me get Forest back, I suggest you offer it now. I'm going to kill you either way, but the degree of pain you suffer will vary depending on what you offer me."

"You heard our conversation, I assume. I don't know anything you don't about where she is. I didn't even think she was still alive. But if you let me live, I'll give you my fealty. I can help you defeat Copernicus," Menjel said quickly.

Syrus pushed him back, disgusted, and punched him full force, in the throat. Menjel clutched at his neck, unable to breathe. He fell to his knees and scrabbled around as he suffocated. Syrus watched, unaffected, as Menjel picked up a shard of Copernicus' shattered sword and attempted but failed to give himself a tracheotomy. He died a nasty shade of plum. Syrus pinched his eyes shut and shook his head. What should he do next?

A groan came from the next room. Syrus followed the sound and found Merhl on the floor, bloodied and coming to from being unconscious. Syrus exhaled in relief and reached to pull Merhl up.

"Are you all right?"

"I think so. I will be soon. I don't know what happened." Merhl shook his head. "I don't remember anything after you telling me to come and get Rahaxeris."

"Rahaxeris is not here, and the other priests are dead. You're lucky to be alive."

"Have you found Forest?" Merhl asked.

"No." Syrus shook his head.

"Please let me continue to help you."

"Thank you. Let's go back to the Onyx castle."

****

Copernicus landed on his back on the deck of the ship in a pool of blood. He held his wounded arm against his wounded chest. The pain shocked him almost as much as the fact that his gashes hadn't pulled together yet. His flesh felt burned where it was cut. With every beat of his heart, blood pumped freely out the holes.

"Shreve!" he yelled.

Shreve came up from below and ran to his side. "What happened, Father?"

"Bind this up!" he ordered through grated teeth.

Shreve took off his shirt and tore it into strips that he tied around Copernicus' forearm and over his chest. "Why aren't you healing? What did this to you?"

"I underestimated Syrus. His power…and the sword he carries…must be neutralized. He poses a real threat to us. To me. And now I've lost Menjel. I'm sure he's dead…" He growled in pain and fury. "I *will* have that sword!"

Shreve looked apprehensively at Copernicus. "I think you need to sleep, for these wounds to heal."

Copernicus got to his feet, hissing in pain. "Perhaps, but right now, I'm just pissed off… This is Forest's fault."

He marched toward the hatch door, his fists clenched tight.

"Uh oh," Shreve said under his breath.

Copernicus shoved the door to Forest's cell aside. She was still unconscious on the floor, Rahaxeris hunched over next to her, his hand on her arm. He knocked Rahaxeris aside and stood over Forest.

76

"Look at this!" Copernicus shouted at her. "Look what your mate did to me!" He slapped her face so hard her whole body rolled to the side with the force.

"Stop!" Rahaxeris yelled.

Copernicus ignored him and grabbed Forest by the shoulders. "Wake up!" he screamed, shaking her violently. "Look at me!"

Her emerald eyes snapped open. She immediately simpered at him. "Please don't hurt me any more, brother."

The hard lines of rage around his eyes eased, and his grip softened on her shoulders. He laid her back down gently on the floor. His blood had soaked through the cloth covering his wounds, and a few drops landed on her face.

"Look at this," he whined, showing her his arm. "Syrus did this to me. It's not healing."

"Got you with my sword, looks like."

Shreve stood in the doorway, his whole body rigid. Rahaxeris glanced at him, feeling as uneasy as Shreve looked.

"It will heal, in time, but not easily, I'm afraid," Forest said.

"Your mate just injured me and dealt my plans a blow. What do you think about that? How does that make you feel?"

Forest frowned, fear gliding under the surface of her eyes. "Well…can you really blame him? He wants me back I'm sure."

Copernicus scowled and tisked. "Evasion." He knelt and looked her over closely, lifting her arm up where he inspected her injection site.

Forest let him, placidly.

"How do you feel physically?" he asked.

77

"Okay, mostly. Why? Are you going to get someone else to kick the shit out of me again?"

He caressed the side of her face. "No. I'm sorry. I didn't know about the baby at the time."

He reached down and stroked Forest's stomach. A spark of red struck out at his hand and shocked him suddenly. He lashed out thoughtlessly at the source of what had caused him pain, pulling his hand back in a fist aimed at the baby. Forest was on her feet faster than a blink, bringing her knee up into Copernicus' face. His head snapped back, his nose gushing blood. He roared and jumped to his feet. He was much bigger and way stronger, but Forest was in a mode she'd never experienced before: mama bear. She'd face down an army of giants with nothing but her teeth and bare hands.

Copernicus' eyes widened at the killing energy coming off Forest. "Stand down," he ordered.

"Try and touch my baby again, and I'll force feed you your own entrails!"

Copernicus swelled. "Is that right?" he growled.

Forest bared her teeth, ready to spring on him. Shreve came up behind her, whacking the hilt of her old sword in the back of her head, knocking her unconscious. He caught her as she went down.

Shreve looked tensely at Copernicus and laughed. "She's quite the wildcat, isn't she?"

"I didn't ask you to interfere," Copernicus snarled.

"Your wounds are looking worse. Brawling is the last thing you need right now. How are you going to march on Halussis bleeding all over like that? Plus I know you're not done with her yet. Haven't your plans been messed up enough today?"

Copernicus sighed. "All right, Shreve. You're right."

He left the room, a trail of blood behind him. Shreve gave Rahaxeris a relived look. Rahaxeris returned his look with one of gratitude. Shreve nodded and left, locking the door after him.

"So what now?" he asked Copernicus as he dressed his wounds.

"I'm going to sleep for a little while and see if that sets me to rights. I want you to go and spread the word to the believers that we will gather tonight at the edge of the Wolf's Wood where the shifter colony used to be."

"Yes, Father. Just the believers? Not the rest?"

"The rest can wait for their orders to come down the chain of command." Copernicus laid down and closed his eyes.

"What about Redge?"

"He's just a slave. Leave him, for now."

Shreve used his ogre blood and opened a portal to Paradigm, where most of the people he needed to contact were hiding.

Chapter Eight

Journey marveled at how she was in the same place again as she had been the previous night. Sitting with her back against the stone wall of the ruin, next to Redge while he slept. She never would have thought she had such self-control. Or maybe the fact that she still hadn't let him know she was right here with him was cowardice and not control. She'd never realized she had masochistic tendencies, for it was real pain to be so close and yet not touch him. She rubbed her arms, shaking her head. It was cowardice.

He stirred. Journey held perfectly still, holding her breath. There was no where she could hide in the hollow space. The only cover she had was the shadow cast from the moonlight over the tree that grew in the center of the house. Redge sighed and opened his eyes. He rolled onto his side and sat up on the bare slats of the bedframe. His elbows rested on his knees, and he put his head in his hands.

Journey's heart beat so hard and fast she was sure he would hear it any second.

He lifted his head and looked right at her. She gasped and rose to her feet, still keeping her back to the wall. He stood, his eyes fathomless. He blinked three times. He raised his hands up, looked at them, and flexed his fingers.

"Strange," his voice was low. "I thought I was awake. I feel awake, but now, I know I'm not."

Her eyes rounded as he came at her slowly. "Yes," she breathed. "You're dreaming."

His breath caught, and he stopped still. "You never speak to me, in my dreams... Not once, have you."

Her whole body was shaking, and her voice was weak through her trembling lips. "You dream of me, Redge?"

He laughed bitterly. "Journey…you haunt me every night. Every *single* night since you left me. Why are you talking to me now?"

"I don't know."

"Perhaps I need you to, now more than ever, because I've lost everyone else." He frowned and looked down at his hands again, rubbing them together. "I feel awake," he whispered.

"You're not. I promise you."

He looked at her slowly and quietly. His eyes hid nothing. She felt the very foundation of her soul shake and begin to crumble. When his eyes filled with tears, she broke completely. Their chemistry turned incendiary.

He reached out. Journey panicked. She couldn't let him touch her. She immediately began to sing, and threw a story into the air between them like a sheer curtain. He stopped and looked at it confusedly, his eyes beginning to dilate as her voice sank into his mind. She couldn't use anything from him because she was determined not to read him. The story she told was her own, taken from her feelings. She had never done such a thing before.

A transparent, younger, life-sized version of her stood between them. The real Journey sang slow, almost whispered notes, more of a hum. His mind gave in to the illusion completely.

"I came back to you, Redge," the Journey-hologram said. "But in a way, I never really left. My heart was always here with you…I've come to warn you you're in terrible danger. Your whole world is in danger."

He hung his head. "You came back to warn me I'm in danger?" he said slowly, his voice sounded drugged. "I hoped you came back to be with me."

"I'm a coward. Remember? Remember how you used to accuse me of that?"

"I can be cruel," he countered. "Remember *you* used to accuse me of that?"

"I never really meant it, Redge."

"I never meant it, either."

He moved to touch the story version, his hand sliding right through her. It didn't faze him. The ghostly Journey reached up and touched his face. He mirrored her action, sliding his thumb over her lips without applying any pressure.

"I was too scared to come back. I was scared of you. Afraid I was too young when I fell for you and it wasn't real. Afraid you had been consumed by the darkness inside you… Afraid of my own darkness."

"You have no darkness, Journey," he argued. "You think only of others and how you can help them."

The hologram shook her head. "That's what I aspire to be, but I'm not. I'm supposed to be selfless. You taught me to care about what *I* wanted. And it was always you. I'm so selfish when it comes to you."

He smiled sleepily. "That's okay…I'll forgive you."

The real Journey smiled, her song halted for a split second. The story remained in the air, but it seemed to have lost a slight hold on him. He stepped back a little and shook his head.

"This dream is heartless," he mumbled. "I want to wake up."

The word heartless stung her. What did he mean by that?

"Why do you want to wake?" her story version asked.

"I want to be free of you, but you never let me go. I'm so sick of this torture. Dreams and fantasies are all I have, and they are not enough.

82

They only leave me with this constant pain… Flesh and blood, that's what I want. Since I can't touch you, I wish you would go away. Leave me to my hopeless desolation and let me go numb to your memory."

"What if you had me again? Not a dream, but me?"

A feral sound rumbled deep in his chest, and the depth of his eyes bottomed out, pulling her down. "I don't think you could handle what I would do to you." His hands clenched. "I don't know if I could handle what would happen…I think if I had you in my arms again…we both might break."

A biting shiver rolled down Journey, and she gasped, her song halted. He blinked. His eyes lost a trace of their sleepiness. She pushed at the story between them, holding it in place. His eyes snapped onto hers, her real eyes, through the haze of the story. He blinked again.

"What are you doing?" he demanded, half lucid.

The illusion was crumbling. She sang a little more forcefully, and his eyes glazed again. She edged along the wall and slipped out through a window frame, into the cool night. She shivered again as she moved away from him through the trees. His words scorched deep inside her. She began to form a plan for the next time she saw him.

Chapter Nine

Rahaxeris woke in the dark, pain vibrating all through him. He felt diseased, on the edge of expiring. His head hung limp on his chest, the cuff around his neck pinched into his chin. His senses were dulled down to a sleepy haze. He lifted his heavy head as a small shuffling sound pushed through his thick mind. The hulking outline of Copernicus leaned over Forest, who was still unconscious on the floor.

"What are you doing?" Rahaxeris demanded, his throat woolen.

"Analyzing," he answered. "Shreve knocked her out hard. She'll have a nasty headache when she wakes. I'm very sorry for it."

"If you love her as you say you do, let her go… You have me."

"No. She needs me. The baby needs me. There's something really wrong here. I'm giving her more Malachi Serum. I don't think the first dose did much of anything."

"It almost killed her. It would have had I not pulled it back out of her. If you give her any more of that, she will, most assuredly die."

Copernicus laughed lightly. "Stop lying. You're not capable of anything with that cuff around your neck. If you could remove the Serum, you would have escaped as well… I'm almost done, now. I think when we get back from our excursion, she will be much better. I think she will be happier to be with me then."

Rahaxeris blinked his blurry eyes and squinted. He felt too weak to respond to the screaming panic inside him as the light from the cracked door glinted off a syringe in Copernicus' hand. If Shreve didn't help her again, this time she would die.

Copernicus moaned deep in his throat and nuzzled Forest's neck. He sank his teeth into her skin, drinking from her for a moment before pulling back and pressing his bloody mouth to hers.

"I'm going to miss her so much over the next few days…" Copernicus stood, dropping the empty syringe on the floor. "Well, Father, are you ready? It's time to leave."

"Where are we going? Where is Shreve?"

"We're going to meet with my followers. They need to see you under my control. Shreve will already be there."

He hauled Rahaxeris up and opened a portal. Forest was left all alone, poisoned yet again. Rahaxeris tried to think his way through the situation. Nothing short of a miracle would save Forest now. His heart prepared for the worst, already beginning to mourn her.

The portal dumped them right in the middle of a raucous party. Torches blazed around the perimeter, illuminating and casting shadows on the hoard of vampires, acting like savages. They pushed around a terrified young she-wolf, taking bites of her randomly. She tried to fight, but there was nothing she could do to escape. Rahaxeris turned away from her as they pounced and began to drain her to death.

Copernicus dragged Rahaxeris to the center of the group and dropped him to the ground in a heap. The blood-crazed, murderous crowd noticed the arrival of their leader.

"Long live King Copernicus! Long live King Copernicus!" they chanted.

Copernicus held up his hand, and they fell silent. "Welcome, my faithful ones! You have my favor. The strike was a tremendous success, thanks to you. We are one step closer to the throne!" he roared.

The group raised their voices along with him.

"You have been very patient. The time is on us again to move forward. Behold!" He gestured to Rahaxeris. "I hold the power of the *Rune-dy*! The high priest is in my total control, and the rest of the *Rune-dy* are dead. Now there is no power to rival ours!"

The crowd shouted in excitement again.

Copernicus waved his hands in a quieting motion. "I am going back to my hideout in Paradigm. Within days, we shall march on Halussis and take the Onyx Castle. I will kill Zeren and re-establish the throne. Regia will once again be as it should be; a kingdom under a sovereign. With me on the throne, the Onyx castle will become the epicenter of a new world order. We will shake the ground from our stronghold. There is not one place or person who will not feel it!"

He paused, looking intently at his followers. "Are you listening carefully to me? Listen well. You have two days to gather the insurgents in your areas. Move them toward Halussis. As of right now, you are on stand-by. Respond to my orders without question or hesitation when they come. The only other voice you listen to is Shreve. If I am not present, Shreve speaks for me. Obey him as you would me… Act faithfully, and I will reward you. The time is now! Go!"

"Long live King Copernicus! Long live King Copernicus!" The chant started again.

****

The serum ran into Forest's blood. It traveled fast up her veins on the way to her heart, where it entered, swirled, and exited back out. The poison flowed down to the baby. Her eyes sprang wide and she gasped, just once. The pain was more than pain. It was a living knife in her blood. Her heart stopped and held fast as though the blood it pumped had turned to thick mud. *No.* Forest brought her hand up and struck herself in the chest. Her heart coughed and pumped again with a terrible effort. She clasped her hands on her stomach and rolled into a ball around her baby.

"Syrus," she whispered before falling back into a death sleep.

****

Zeren, Ithiel, Merick, Netriet, Kindel, and Ena stood around a table laid with a map of Regia, trying to figure where Forest might be. Zeren had dispatched search parties of royal soldiers, each led by one of the Kata masters that came with Syrus to the castle after the mountain was attacked.

There were many ideas being thrown around the table about where she might be hidden.

Syrus strode into the room with Merhl, and everyone fell silent. None of them needed to ask if he'd found her; they could tell by the look on his face.

"The *Rune-dy* are dead, except Rahaxeris. Copernicus has him," Syrus said. "Copernicus plans to keep Forest alive so she can sit on the throne next to him…" He took a deep breath, schooling his rage before continuing. "Despite that I heard him say this, Forest has already been on the edge of death since she was taken…" He rubbed the heel of his hand over his heart and grimaced. "I'd given up hope. I thought I'd lost her…We can't rely on his intentions to keep her alive. We have to get her back. But I fought him. I can defeat him. He would be dead now, if he hadn't run like a coward."

Everyone looked around at each other.

Kindel slammed his fist down on the table. "If only we still had Redge," he said.

"Redge is lost to us!" Syrus growled.

"What haven't we thought of yet?" Ena demanded.

Netriet's eyes rounded, and her cheeks flushed. "No one has sought out Shi!" She moved over to Merhl; Merick followed her. "Send us to the Wolf's Wood," she said to Merhl urgently. "Shi might be able to help us."

87

"Wait," Zeren said. "Take some backup with you."

He gestured for the security ogres standing at the door to come forward. Netriet, Merick, and two ogres went through the portal Merhl opened.

Syrus clasped at his chest and fell onto his knees. Kindel and Zeren ran to him and braced him by the shoulders.

"It's happening again!" Syrus yelled. "Forest is dying! We have to hurry…no time…her heart fails…"

None of them could do anything to help Syrus. They had no answers, could offer no comfort.

He got to his feet and looked at the map, but his mind couldn't focus. All he could do was feel. Forest's life was going, and again, he was out of time to save her. Whatever was happening to her, it was happening faster than before, much faster. All hope left him. She only had moments left. There wasn't time to do anything. He had no direction. It was over... He'd lost her.

"Send me home, Merhl," Syrus said quietly.

Tears filling his large eyes, Merhl nodded and opened a portal for Syrus.

"Go with him," Zeren told Merhl.

Merhl came through the portal after Syrus. He stood back and was silent, forced to witness Syrus' anguish.

Syrus fell out onto his knees. He threw his head back to the sky. "FOREST!"

His voice echoed for miles. The terrible sound falling again and again with the piercing agony of his soul. He struck the ground with his fist. Lightning shot through the earth and rocks. A tremor rolled through the area in a terrible aftershock. He sighed raggedly and pulled Forest's sword from its scabbard.

"What are you doing?" Merhl asked.

"I'm getting ready to die."

"No… Don't do that." Merhl came forward.

Syrus jumped to his feet, turning the blade to Merhl. Merhl stopped, assaulted by the look in Syrus' eyes. He couldn't stand the pain he saw there. He understood clearly the desire to be free of that kind of suffering. Merhl held his hands up and took a step back.

"You will be missed, Syrus. Regia will mourn the loss of you and Forest."

Syrus lowered the blade away from Merhl. "Go home…make sure Forest's memory is never forgotten."

Merhl tried to clear the lump in his throat, but it wouldn't budge. With his heart heavier than it had ever been, he bowed to Syrus and opened a portal back to the Onyx castle.

Syrus watched the portal close and sighed. He looked around the garden. His memories stroked his heart with soft fingers that soothed, and the next moment stabbed deep with razor-sharp nails. He had nothing to live for. Without Forest there was no reason to continue. He couldn't move on. He couldn't heal. Nothing could replace his mate or his child. The excruciation was already there inside him, waiting. It hovered, letting Syrus know it had him, and there was no escape.

"At least I had you…even if it was such a short time…moments really. I wouldn't change it, my love. I only wish we'd had more time…" He pointed the tip of the blade to his chest and held still, listening to Forest's heart. He could feel the moment was upon him. Any second, and her heart would beat its last. The moment she died, so would he.

Chapter Ten

Everyone had left, except Shreve. Copernicus had taken Rahaxeris with him to Paradigm, and the believers were all gone to gather the slaves and make ready for the takeover of the Onyx castle. Shreve sighed as he put out the torches and worked to erase the traces of the gathering. He hated his life. He didn't believe in anything. He was just along for the ride. Doing what he was told. There was so much innocent blood on his hands. Had this been his purpose, when he'd been created? To be a weapon? He didn't want to be a weapon. But he didn't know what he did want to be.

He was almost finished clearing the area, but he had one more job left: taking care of the body of the girl that had died for sport. He'd been avoiding going near her, but he had to now. Her eyes were open, unseeing, directed at the moon. She was young, in that age right before maturity. Beautiful. And her life had ended before it really began.

"I'm sorry," he whispered. "May your soul find peace."

"Sophie!" A cry came up behind him.

Shreve turned to see a young woman running at him. She looked just like the girl on the ground. He stepped back as she fell on the dead one, who was surely her sister. The young woman wailed and held the body to her chest. She looked at Shreve and stood. Challenge seared through the pain on her tear-streaked face. Hatred flamed in her deep purple eyes. She pulled her long light brown hair back from her face. He couldn't help but admire her trim, powerful build.

"Are you the killer?" she demanded.

"No, but I didn't help her, either."

"You're one of them, aren't you? The Aluka circle?"

"Yes," he said quietly.

Her fists clenched. "I am no one, *yet*. But someday, I will stop all of you. If the rest of Regia cannot stop you, then the wolves will. And I will lead them."

Shreve smiled. He liked her. "Good luck to you then. My condolences on your loss. What is your name?"

"Sabra, and don't you forget it."

"I can assure you, I won't."

Shreve gave her a little bow and opened a portal. The dead girl would be taken care of properly. He was sorry to see she had been loved, that she would be missed. She had family…a sister. He had a sister too, who needed his help. And Copernicus was elsewhere.

Shreve landed on the deck of the ship and went directly below to Forest's cell.

"Forest? Forest are you awake yet?" He came to her side.

His spine stiffened as his eyes adjusted to the dimness. He grabbed her arm. "Damn it, Father."

Forest's veins were dark grey and swelled like exposed tree roots from the injection site. He laid his head against her chest and listened. This was beyond him. He didn't have any special power or skill set that could help her. Shreve contemplated for a second. Saving her life might cost him his.

Screw it, he thought as he shifted his appearance so he didn't resemble Copernicus and opened a portal.

****

Syrus heard the portal open, thinking it was Merhl again. He opened his eyes slowly and blinked once, sure he was imagining what was in front of him. Syrus rushed to the stranger who carried Forest and took her into his arms. He looked at the deliverer, but the man had already turned and was going back through the open portal. He hadn't even gotten a good look at him. Then the portal closed, leaving them alone.

He laid Forest down gently on the ground and took both of her hands. The pull of their bond mixed with his mage power in his palms. Red light moved up from his hands into hers and rolled through her whole body before coming back to Syrus, translating to him what was going on inside her.

A small lightning-filled sphere formed in his hand, and he placed it on the crook of Forest's arm. The sphere began to spin and turn grey. It slowed and stopped. He grabbed it, now filled with poison pulled from her, and threw it. It exploded when it hit the ground. Syrus made another sphere, again placing it on her arm. *If only she wasn't so far gone.*

Syrus removed every drop of the toxin from her body, but the damage it caused left her bludgeoned inside. He felt her slip deeper into death sleep, her heart too tired, too injured to continue. The muscles of the walls and chambers sighed in defeat, having lost all structural integrity, and let go of the blood inside it like a fist relaxing open.

"Oh no you don't! Forest, you come back here, right now!"

Syrus closed his eyes. Rage beyond what he had felt on the Obsidian Mountain when he'd lit it up and killed the attacking ogres, pooled under his ribs. She was right here. He wouldn't let her die. It was non-negotiable.

Another lightning-filled sphere formed over his heart. He pulled it off and slammed it into Forest's chest. The sphere thrust through her flesh and bones, into her expired heart where it broke open.

Her eyes shot open for a second then rolled back again closed, her heart coughing weakly once just once.

He pressed his forehead against hers. "Fight, Forest! Fight!" he shouted. "When have you ever backed down from anything?! I'll never forgive you, if you give up now! Do you hear me? I will never forgive you!"

He held her against his chest. A dome of red electricity covered them. Tendrils of it latched on to Forest, shocking her over and over. In one last push, Syrus gave her the full force of everything he had, putting his own life in danger with the effort.

The dome blazed in a blinding flash and pulled back down into Syrus before shooting through her like a shockwave.

He couldn't feel anything; he could barely hold on to her. He slumped down as she took a shallow breath. Then another. Her tattered heart beat faintly, and she opened her eyes.

"I didn't know you could be so mean," she whispered.

Relief didn't begin to cover what he felt. He chuckled. He had his family in his arms. He would have thought it a dream, had he not hurt so much.

Tears filled his eyes. "Don't you ever…ever scare me like that again."

With great effort, she reached up slowly and placed her hand on her stomach. "I'm pregnant."

"I know… I can hear the baby's heartbeat, just as I can hear yours."

"Is the baby okay?"

He frowned, listening. What did he know about babies? The sound of the baby's pulse was different than it had been before, but it was steady. "I don't know," he said honestly.

She blinked and looked around as much as she could without moving her head at all. "Home? How did I get here? Rahaxeris?"

Syrus shook his head. "Someone brought you. I didn't get a good look at him. He left as soon as I had you, without saying a word."

Forest frowned and then closed her eyes. "I can hardly move." She groaned with pain and gingerly touched her sternum. "What did you do to me?"

He kissed her mouth, his tears falling on her cheeks. "What I had to."

Syrus took a deep breath, mustering the strength to stand, and carried her into the house. He barely made it to the bed and laid her down before his legs gave out. He fell onto the bed and wrapped his arms around her in a vise grip before passing out.

****

Zeren was beside himself. At first Merhl wouldn't talk. When he finally did, Zeren was utterly torn about what to do. He wanted to go to Syrus and demand that he not harm himself. The only thing that held him back was his firsthand experience of losing his own life mate. Zeren had decided to continue living because of Syrus. If he were in Syrus' position now, having lost his mate and his baby at the same time…well, despite how it would hurt Zeren to lose Syrus, he didn't want him to live with that kind of agony.

Zeren closed himself away in his quiet room and sat still in the dark. He waited one hour before going back to the room where those who cared most about Forest had just stood, trying to help save her. Netriet and Merick were back and someone had obviously told them Forest was dead. Merick stared at the floor with empty eyes as Netriet clung to him. Kindel held on to Ena and stroked her back as she sobbed on his chest. Merhl looked at the floor, crying silently. And Ithiel sat in a chair with his eyes closed, meditating through whatever he was feeling.

"Open a portal for me," Zeren said quietly to Merhl. "Leave it open, I'll be back after I see to my son's body."

He walked slowly through the rushing blackness, pushed onward by duty and weighed down with sorrow. The garden was empty. Zeren looked around. The ground in front of him was scorched in a perfect circle. He frowned as he noticed the door on the house stood open. He walked into the silent space and listened. He heard breathing. Zeren followed the sound into the bedroom. How could it be?

Both of them were there. Zeren exhaled in relief as all the grief he'd been feeling vanished. He shook his head in amazement. It wasn't the first time Zeren had thought that Forest and Syrus were more than destined life mates, more than desperately in love with each other, they had something so rare and strong he didn't even have a name to put to it, but it seemed to create miracles.

They looked terrible, but they were alive. He'd have to wait to get the story. They definitely needed rest.

Zeren ran back to the waiting portal to tell everyone he'd left grieving, that their tears were unneeded.

Chapter Eleven

Shreve stood on the deck of the ship, looking out at the sea. He was supposed to be making sure everyone was getting ready for the takeover of the Onyx Castle. He shook his head and ran his fingers through his hair. Learning he was a clone had changed things for him. Copernicus wasn't his father as he'd been led to believe. That simple fact had altered something inside him. He owed Copernicus nothing.

He had the power of every Regian race, but he probably wouldn't live a normal lifespan. His DNA was old from the moment he was created. But on the other hand, he had been spliced with wizard blood as well. Who knew? He might outlive everyone.

He didn't know who he was, but he wanted to. He hadn't begun his life in Regia, but it was his home. There would be a place for him, somewhere. He could hide in the open for the rest of his life, if he wanted. He could change his face, and he could change race at a moment's notice. He could do anything he wanted with his life.

His life, he thought for the very first time. This was his life, and he would claim it.

Shreve pulled Forest's silver sword from around his waist. He thought about her as he looked at the blade. Had her mate been able to save her life? The child's life? He would find out later. He slid the sword back into its scabbard. Maybe one day, he'd return it to her.

His gaze traveled down to the wooden planks under his feet. It was time to sink this ship and for him to disappear before the window of opportunity closed. He went below deck into Forest's empty cell. Shifting his right arm into beast form, Shreve punched a hole straight through the floor. Water rushed in. He quickly punched three more holes. The water rose up to his chest. He smiled to himself as he shifted his arm back, pulling from his ogre blood, and opened a portal. He went through the rushing blackness as the ship sank beneath the jagged surface of the Crystalline Sea.

****

Redge was disoriented. The morning sunlight fell on his face through the open roof of the ruin. He sat up, groaning. He ran his hand over his slave mark, wishing he could cut it out of his flesh, but he knew attempting that would do no good. Only when Copernicus was dead would he regain his freedom. He'd been such a fool, thinking he could go in and make a real difference in the effort to take Copernicus out. The price of his folly was beyond any nightmare he'd ever had. His hands had been turned against his friends and against his loyalty to Regia.

Acidic misery moved slowly through him as he thought about when Syrus had come to see him. His mind lingered on the things he didn't want to think about: Copernicus marking him, beating Forest, the unborn child she carried, what torture Syrus must be going through, if Forest was even still alive? And now, in the midst of all that, he'd dreamed about Journey in a way he never had before.

She'd spoken to him. She'd touched him. It had been so intense, so real, and as a side effect, his heart delivered self-inflicted wounds to the rest of him with every pulse. The tangible layers of the dream had made him miss her more. He always missed her, but at the moment, he raged for her. He was so ravenous for her, so miserable and utterly unsatisfied.

He stood and sighed. His stomach rolled with hunger. How long had it been since he'd eaten anything? He'd have to go into the city. He didn't want to chance running into anyone he knew. He had nothing to hide his face with, no hooded cloak. He reached into his pocket and pulled out the contents. Just a few coins. Enough to stop into a smaller, seedy hotel for a while. He could bathe, eat, and head back to his isolation before midday.

He shouldn't do it, he thought. His stomach growled again, vociferously, making up his mind for him. He headed for Halussis, hoping desperately he could get in and get out without being noticed by anyone who would recognize him.

Every last coin was spent on the room, bath, and food. But he'd also managed to pick up a cheap set of clothes from a street merchant. He didn't have time to launder his clothes, and the thought of putting his dirty ones back on after his bath was abhorrent. It had only taken him an hour to clean up and eat. Now, he was anxious to get away from the public.

Redge stepped out of the hotel into the side street and was immediately knocked roughly in the shoulder by a running, young man.

"Where's the fire?" Redge yelled.

The young man stopped for a second and turned back to look at him. His eyes were excited, and he was panting from running. "There's a Storyteller! Just a block over. My brother told me! Come on!" He waved for Redge to follow and took off again.

Redge's feet had grown roots right through the street. *Storyteller.*

Both his mind and his heart stalled. It wasn't her. It wasn't possible. She couldn't come back. It was someone else from her world. He uprooted his feet and moved in the direction the young man had gone. Maybe this person knew Journey. Maybe he could ask about her, and if this Storyteller decided to go home, perhaps they would be willing to take her a message from him. He hardly dared hope for so much.

Redge rounded the corner. A group of people huddled around the Storyteller. Again, his feet grew roots. He shook himself. It was a mirage. He was projecting his memories onto the woman in the center of the mesmerized crowd. She had her back to him, but the way she held herself...he knew it so well. The sunlight caressed her golden brown skin and glinted off the small metal baubles laced randomly through her braided hair. Her voice moved over him. He could barely hear it at this distance…but still…

Redge shook himself again. It was impossible. Perhaps this person was related to Journey. He looked at the story, moving in the center of the crowd, and a punch hit him in the gut. There in the mists of the story he saw himself as a young man. It was him! He was in the story, and then so was Journey. The Storyteller told the dazed crowd about their tragic love.

He moved closer, unable to stop himself, until he was standing on the edge of the group. He could hear her voice clearly now, but she still had her back to him. It wasn't possible, he told himself again, firmly.

"Journey?" he whispered.

The song stopped. She turned, her magenta eyes locking onto his. The entire universe held still. He couldn't think of what to say, or what to do. There was no calculation, flirtation, testing, or games. He did what he had to, that was all. He reached forward and grabbed her by the hand.

They left the city, hand in hand, in silence.

****

They walked all the way back to the ruin. Her heart had been holding still for so long, but now it began to rouse from its sleep. Her hand ached in his. This first physical contact after so long was dreadfully powerful, intoxicating.

As soon as he had her through the door, he turned on her. Violent shivers pricked all the way down her insides. Her breath came in and out, quickly and shallow. He took both of her hands in his. His whole body trembled. His gaze pushed hard and deep into hers. Everything had changed…and nothing had changed.

One single tear slid from his eye, and he took a sharp breath. He raised her hands to his lips, kissing each of them in turn. Then her palms, wrists, forearms. He kissed her up to her collarbone and sank his teeth into her neck.

"Redge," she exhaled raggedly. "Talk to me."

"No," he growled. "You told me everything last night."

"But you've told me nothing."

He pulled back a bit and looked in her eyes again. "Ask me quickly."

"Do you still love me?"

"Don't you know? Haven't you read it in my broken heart?"

"Do you want me to read it?"

He kissed her roughly, his chest pressed forcefully against hers. "Read it."

She did then, finally. It choked her. Her throat went thick, and she couldn't breathe as she felt what her leaving had done to him all those years ago, and that he had no hope to ever see her again. She had suffered acutely, but his was the greater pain. He loved without reservation. He loved her fully, with everything he was, and it had never dimmed. She'd feared in vain, for there wasn't even the faintest trace of those kind of feelings inside him for another. Reading him left her staggered. How could he love her this much, still, after all this time?

"Well?" he demanded.

She nodded her head in a few quick jerks. "All right... You said we would both break, if you got your hands on me again."

A faint trace of the cocky youth she'd fallen in love with flashed in his expression. "Scared?"

"No," she whispered. "I'm ready to break."

Her heart nearly jumped free of her ribcage as he leaned in and kissed her mouth. She remembered this. One second of sweetness… then rushed the insatiable insanity. Empty years of being apart raged and demanded to be filled up right then. It couldn't be fast enough. She held onto him and turned her face to the sky. Her body remembered his, and it seemed his remembered hers. Oh, she broke all right. She broke, and so did he.

"This is impossible." He panted, looking down at her.

"I'm sorry, it took me so long… Coming back wasn't impossible, it was however, very, *very* difficult."

He kissed her again, his eyes open, pouring his soul into hers. The first wave of reuniting had been violent in its intensity, ravenous, and irrational, now replaced by a sweet ache that demanded to savor everything slowly. She sighed into him, but he pulled away, a terrible look on his face. He ran his hands through his long hair and turned his back on her. Her body ached with losing the contact of his.

"Redge?"

"Why did you have to come back now?"

Anger flashed. "Don't play games with me! Don't even think about it. I was just inside your heart. I know you love me more than your own life."

He swore angrily. "I mean, *now.* All these years, the way I've lived for you…I'm a good man. I've been a soldier, a captain, an investigator. I've lived in the Onyx Castle. Prince Syrus is—*was*—my best friend. I rose above my origins and have lived with dignity. I wish you could have come back to see me like that. But now…I'm a slave to an evil man. I've lost everything. I've never been so debased, and this is how you have to come back to me…I have nothing to offer you. I have nothing. You probably don't even believe me."

She sighed and went to him, grabbing him by the shoulders. "I believe you. I believe you were all those things. And I'm proud of you… Can you not get back what you lost?"

He shook his head. "I don't know. I doubt it."

She touched the slave mark on his neck. "It can be undone?"

"Only when my master is dead. And I don't have the power to kill him… He's made me do terrible things, Journey."

She pursed her lips and looked down at his chest. When she'd read him before she was only looking for one thing. This time, she would see everything else. She absorbed what she learned with a heavy heart. But her healing instinct quickly took over her sorrow. She began to plot how to help him, and an idea flashed in her mind. Maybe, just maybe…

"Are you too proud to let me help you?" she asked.

He frowned and shook his head. "I've no pride left."

"Really?" A small smile curved her lips. "I would think any man who could do to a woman what you just did to me would have a great amount of pride."

He chuckled, the heaviness on him easing a little. "I love you, Journey."

"Then let me help you. Let me try."

"What do you think you can do?"

"What happens to you when your master forces his will on you?" she asked.

"He gives an order—it doesn't have to be verbal—and I turn into a puppet. I cannot stop myself from carrying it out. My hands belong to him."

"Does your mind go blank when this happens?"

"No. I wish it did. I am perfectly aware of everything I am doing but powerless to stop myself. Only when the order is lifted or fulfilled do I regain control of my body."

"Good... That's good," she said, looking off at nothing.

"That's good?"

"Yes. I think it is. I think, if I were with you when you received an order, if you let me in, I could give you the power to override it."

"You mean you'll hypnotize me with a story?" He frowned.

"Sort of."

"Well, let's try it. I'm under an order right now to stay in Halussis until Shreve comes to get me."

She smiled. "All right, let's take a walk and see how far away from Halussis we can get."

They headed out hand in hand, but when they reached the open doorway Journey dug in her heels. He turned to her questioningly.

"Not just yet. I need to be broken again... right now." She pulled him back inside.

Chapter Twelve

Syrus watched Forest intently. She continued to sleep, but sleep was all it was. She wasn't in any danger now. She was healing. Her heart was still very weak, but it was growing stronger by the hour. He sat next to the bed and stared at her as though she might vanish if he turned away for even a second. He touched her gently, kissed her face, and laid his head on her stomach.

His power was in the baby. He could feel the new life surge and snap with his red lightning current. It was the first time he was able to feel calm about the child since he'd first heard their little heartbeat quicken. His heart swelled. He was a father. The thought made him dizzy. Who were they? What would they become? Half vampire, one fourth elf, one fourth shifter. What amazing gifts. They would literally be one of a kind.

He imagined a son and how wonderful it would be to train his boy in the Kata. Then he imagined a girl with her mother's beauty and strength. Oh, shit, that would be trouble.

His eyes slid out of focus as he got lost in his thoughts of fatherhood.

"Syrus."

Forest's hushed voice broke through his reverie. He blinked and looked down at her, taking her hand and kissing it.

"How are you feeling?"

"Terrible." She placed her hands on her stomach. "I'm so drained. I've no strength at all."

"It's okay. You just need some more time. It's a good thing you're so tough, otherwise you wouldn't have survived."

Her eyebrows pulled down as she traced a gentle line along the side of his eye. "What happened to you? You've changed."

He looked away from her, self-conscious. "Sorry. I've noticed a difference in the way people look at me, the way they treat me. It doesn't frighten you, does it? I couldn't stand that."

"I could never fear you, my love. But I can see why others do. You emanate warning."

"Good." His voice was sharp.

She smiled weakly. "What happened to you?" she asked again.

"Rage. I thought I knew rage, but I was wrong. It was rage that transformed me into a mage, and now it has transformed me into something else." He frowned at her. "Do I look bad to you?"

She snorted and then sobered. "No, not at all. I like that others find it off putting. Maybe it's just me and that's good, but you are way too hot, Syrus. I don't want to let you out in public."

He pressed his lips against hers softly, but it still hurt. He felt her pain response and pulled away.

"Tell me what's going on? Has Copernicus shown his face? Is there any fighting?"

"I don't know. And I'm not leaving you to find out, so don't ask."

She smiled feebly and then groaned. "I need some water."

"Okay. The kitchen is as far as I go from your side. Even that will be a struggle."

Syrus propped her up on a few extra pillows and left the bedroom to get her a drink. He jumped in alarm and swore loudly as he entered the living room. Zeren sat quietly in the corner.

"Damn it, Dad! You startled me! I didn't know you were here."

"So I gathered." Zeren smiled, standing and pulling his son into a tight hug. "I've been through a hell of a day, Syrus. I thought I'd lost all of you."

"You almost did. Very nearly."

"Syrus?" Forest called from the bedroom.

Syrus frowned at Zeren. "She's very weak."

"I won't wear her out," Zeren said as he went in to see Forest.

Syrus got the water and came back into the bedroom and stopped on the threshold, watching his father hug his mate. "You take your time and get well. I've set up a guard for you. You'll be safe. We won't lose you again."

"Security ogres?" she asked.

"Just Merhl. The rest are volunteers, well Merhl volunteered, too. Demanded to protect you is more like it." Zeren smiled. "Ithiel, Merick, Netriet, and Kindel all insisted they would take turns guarding you."

"Kindel needs to be at work," Forest argued.

"You can boss him around when you see him. Don't worry about anything else right now."

Sad lines pulled around her eyes. "The Fair?"

"Don't worry. Your friends are fine. Only minor injuries."

Forest exhaled in relief. Zeren kissed her head and left the room. Syrus set her water on the table next to her and followed his father out into the garden.

"Thank you," Syrus said quietly. "For lying to her about the Fair."

Zeren grimaced and nodded. "I hated that I had to. You're right—she's alarmingly weak. She can't handle that right now...I didn't want to ask, but..."

"What?" Syrus asked.

"Did the baby survive?"

Syrus smiled. "Yes."

Zeren hugged Syrus again tightly. "Good! I'm so relieved you didn't lose them, either of them. Forest will get better. We'll fix this trouble Regia is in. The world must be safe for my grandchild!" Zeren let go and made to leave. "Merhl is just outside the gate. He's waiting to create a new level of security over your home."

"Thank you. Please send Ithiel here soon. We need to keep working on our plans to counteract Copernicus, and I can't leave Forest, guard or not. I have to stay close to her."

"Of course. I've called all the masters and search parties back. Everywhere is on high alert. The wolves have been keeping to themselves, but just this morning, a new ambassador showed up at the castle: a young she-wolf, claiming to be gaining in power in the pack. They are ready to join with the rest of Regia in this fight, even though they were not targeted in the strike."

Syrus frowned. "I'm sure this is a stupid question, but you did make *totally* sure they are who they say they are and not one of Copernicus'?"

"We're sure."

Merhl opened a portal for Zeren, and he left.

"So," Syrus asked the ogre. "What are we going to do to make sure Forest is secure?"

Merhl rubbed his twisted hands together. "I'm going to create something new. Something I've never done before…I want to try and make a blood lock. Only those whose blood I have can enter the dome I'm going to create. I already have Zeren's, Ithiel's, Merick's, Netriet's, and Kindel's blood. Now I just need yours."

"Interesting. How much blood?"

"Just a drop." Merhl pulled out a small knife.

Syrus cut a line on his index finger and held the wound over Merhl's open palm. He caught the blood and closed his hand over it.

"Can the lock be broken?" Syrus asked.

"Anything can be broken, but I'm building in many layers to safeguard failure."

Syrus nodded. "When will it be finished?"

"In a few moments. You will hear it."

Syrus went back into the house, anxious to get back to Forest's side. He did indeed hear the blood lock close over them. The sound was like the slamming of a heavy vault door. Forest was asleep again. The warmth of a fever began building under her skin, and splotchy red patches spread over her cheeks.

Syrus put his head in his hands. She would be all right, he told himself forcefully. She would be all right.

****

Redge could scarcely stop looking at Journey, afraid the whole day had been a dream. He almost tripped more than a few times because he wasn't looking where he was going, he just looked at her. The light of sunset breathed on her russet skin and glinted in her magenta eyes. She

108

was so exotically breathtaking, and she was his… At least for now. He hadn't yet asked her if she was able to stay, too afraid of the answer.

His slave mark began to bite down and burn as they neared the rural limits of Halussis. They reached the invisible line, and his body locked down. He could take a step backward, but in front of him was a wall.

"Is it happening?" she asked.

"Yes. I can't move forward at all. And my slave mark burns."

"Try to defy the order on your own."

"I have." His voice was emphatic. "Many times, with previous orders, ones I wanted to ignore much more than this, I can assure you. It's pointless."

"Just try," she said gently. "I need to see it."

He took a deep breath and closed his eyes. He didn't know what to do. He thought about walking forward, pushing his body, straining to move it. Pain rushed into his muscles, and sweat beaded on his skin from the effort. Nothing happened, just a faint tremor shook deep inside him. He stopped pushing and opened his eyes.

Journey stared intently at his chest, her eyes tunneled, and a look of concentration pulled on her brow. He held still and waited.

"Clear your mind of me," she said finally.

He laughed. "How?"

She returned his smile indulgently. "Focus all of yourself on moving past the boundary. Let your one and only desire be to leave Halussis. I'm going to join with you on this. Don't worry about me or what I'm doing, just focus on walking forward."

He exhaled and looked forward, concentrating on what she'd said, and tried again to move forward. It felt the same for the first few seconds, like he was shoved up against a wall. Her voice came low from behind him, the notes sliding deep into his mind. Heat snaked up and under the back of his skull, moved through his head, and broke out of his eyes. His sight opened wider, his irises expanding around the warmth.

The invisible wall trembled. He placed his hands flat on it and pushed. His whole body shook with the effort. The weight was too much for him. He pushed harder.

"Stop!" Journey said loudly. "You'll give yourself an aneurism."

He sighed, dejected, and turned around to face her. He reached to take her in his arms, but she evaded his grasp. She smiled, sidestepped him, and walked through the barrier that held him.

"Hey," he protested.

Her smile widened. "I'm just trying to give your resolve a different direction… Don't you want to come and get me?"

"You're playing a dangerous game, woman."

She laughed and took another step away. "Come on." She licked her lips slowly. "Don't you want me?" Her voice dropped to a seductive whisper.

He narrowed his eyes at her and geared up again to push against the wall. She began to hum again, just one long low note, and his vision clouded around the edges. His burning slave mark cooled and tingled. His hands pushed into the wall. The solidness of it softened, but it still held.

Look at me, her voice sounded in his mind.

She turned her head slowly to the side, her hand ran down the side of her face and pulled her hair over one shoulder, giving him a full view of her long, lovely neck. She kept her head turned to the side, but her eyes cut to his. *Come on…*

His slave mark went numb as the wall broke open. He caught her against him and kissed her roughly.

"You did it, Redge."

He shook his head. "No, you did. If I weren't so hot for you, you'd terrify me…You have such strange power, Storyteller."

She touched his scar. "I don't know if its hold has gone dead or just weakened. We need to test it some more. Did your master give you any other orders?"

He thought for a moment. "I was told not to contact anyone from my past, and…" His eyes suddenly went wide and wild. "I have to tell Syrus where Forest is! I know I can now!"

He grabbed her by the hand and ran. He ran faster than he ever had before. It took hours, but he didn't slow even once, and Journey kept pace with him and didn't waste her breath asking him questions.

They arrived close to the parameter of Forest and Syrus' property in the middle of the night and finally stopped, exhausted and out of breath. Redge pushed ahead and ran again into an invisible wall. This wall wasn't one in his mind, it was real, and it held Journey back as well.

She put her hands on it and frowned. The next second, red sparks shocked both of her palms. She jumped back and whimpered in pain.

"Are you all right?"

"I think so," she said.

Redge backed up a step from the wall. "Syrus!" he shouted as loudly as he could. "Let me in! I know where Forest is! I can tell you now! I'll take you there!"

A shadow came up from the other side of the wall, like it traveled through the water. It slowly grew more solid, and Kindel stepped through the wall. Redge grabbed him by the shoulder. He'd never been so happy to see him. Kindel shoved him backward and pulled a sword on him.

"Get back!" Kindel ordered. "I don't want to have to kill you!"

"Kindel, it's me! I need to find Syrus. It's urgent! I have to tell him where Forest is."

Kindel's face crumpled with confusion, and he looked at Journey and then back to Redge. "You're one of them. Copernicus sent you here, didn't he?"

"No! Look, this is Journey. She's a Storyteller. She helped me break through my obedience to the slave mark Copernicus gave me. I know where Forest is! We have to save her!"

Kindel narrowed his eyes at Redge. "I can't trust you."

"Please!" he bellowed. "Tell Syrus—"

"Forest is no longer a captive of Copernicus. Your message, if it was trustworthy, comes too late. Now leave. Don't force my hand."

The rejection was bitterly painful even though he understood it. Redge took Journey's hand and began to leave.

"Redge," Kindel called after him.

He turned and looked back.

"I'm sorry."

Chapter Thirteen

Kindel moved back through the blood lock and approached the stone house. He knocked lightly, hoping the sound wouldn't wake Forest. He really didn't want to evoke Syrus' anger. He'd turned so frighteningly protective. Kindel understood. Had he been in Syrus' shoes, he'd have been just as protective. But Syrus was scary as hell now. Different, more powerful, and more deadly than ever.

The lightning blaze in his eyes had banked now that he had Forest back, but the embers were still there, ready and waiting to ignite into a firestorm.

Kindel knocked again softly, and after a few seconds, Syrus opened the door. Kindel stepped back from the intensity radiating off of him. Irritation and worry pulsed from him.

"What?" he asked through clenched teeth. "What's wrong?"

"Redge was just here. Outside the blood lock, raving that he had to talk to you, that he could tell you now where Forest was."

Syrus frowned but didn't speak.

"He had someone with him, a woman. He said she was a Storyteller and she had helped free him from his slave mark... She wasn't Regian, I know that for sure. But I sent him away. It could be fake. Copernicus might be trying to get him close to Forest so he can take her again. He could just be following orders. I...really wanted to believe him, but I thought it too risky."

"You did well... The woman, did he tell you her name?"

"Journey."

Syrus sighed and looked down. "Okay. Thanks Kindel."

"What should I do if he comes back?"

"Don't answer. Just stay under the lock. I need a little time to think about it."

"How is she?" Kindel inquired about Forest.

"Feverish."

Kindel took a step back. "I'll let you get back to her. Netriet will be coming in when I leave at dawn. I know she really wanted to talk to Forest."

"If Forest is awake, I'll let her. But if you talk to her first, let her know we're not telling Forest about the Fair just yet."

"Yes. Of course."

****

Syrus closed the door and leaned against it. Redge showing up was a sting. While he'd been keeping vigil next to Forest, his mind had wandered to Redge a few times. Each time he thought about him, Syrus felt either anger or regret, but mostly anger. What he and Forest had gone through was still way too new. Too painful, too vivid.

His mind brought back old memories. Things Redge had told him many, many years ago. About the Storyteller, Journey. Redge hadn't told Syrus the details of what happened between them, but he did remember that she had left him, and Redge found speaking about her painful. He'd loved her.

He remembered teasing Redge about one of his mother's courtiers having her eye on him. Redge showed no interest, even though the young woman was beautiful and would have been an easy conquest. He seemed neither embarrassed, flattered, nor keen in any way. Redge never showed

114

an interest in romantic relationships of any kind. He was a good friend to those he chose to be friends with, and that was all.

So, if Kindel was right, the only one who had ever interested him was back in his life.

"Syrus," Forest moaned from the bedroom.

He ran to her, anxious because she was finally awake again. He took her hand, feeling a wave of relief at her cooling temperature. "You're better."

She nodded, looking intently into his eyes. Relief built another layer. Her eyes were still bloodshot, but they were clear. She was really awake, and she was coherent. Bruises had blossomed all over her, discoloring her skin. He smoothed her hair back from her forehead.

"What's happening?" she asked. "Has Copernicus made a move?"

"No. Not yet."

"He has my father. He's hobbled him. We have to rescue him."

"There is no 'we' in this equation, Forest. As much as I'm sure you hate it, *you* can't do anything, right now... Can you tell me what happened to you? What did you learn while you were with Copernicus?"

"I'll tell you after you get me some food. Your baby is hungry."

Syrus smiled and placed his hand on her stomach. A small mound curved up into his palm. Wonder and awe filled him. The baby was growing *really* fast.

He'd never seen Forest eat so much, but he guessed that was another good sign her health was returning. When she was finished, she rubbed her stomach with both hands.

"Pregnancy is weird," she said. "And...terrifying to be honest, for many reasons."

"Are you not happy at all about it?" he asked gently.

Tears instantly began running down her cheeks.

"Hey, what's this?" His voice was soothing.

"I'm so scared. I've never felt fear this intense before. I would have been scared even if I hadn't been kidnapped, because this baby is so mixed. It worries me. I'm afraid for them. I know all too well that they will be ostracized. Probably not as badly as I have been, but still. And then..." Her breathing became fast and panicked. "Then, the poison... What kind of damage has that done? I did my best to protect the baby while I was being beaten, but even then, I..."

Forest was distracted from her fear by the look that crossed Syrus' face.

"What is it?" she asked. "Why do you look so murderous?"

"Redge," he hissed through his teeth.

"Hey, look at me!" she ordered. "You have to let go of that. Don't you dare hold that against him."

His look of fury didn't falter.

"You don't know what it's like to be a slave, Syrus. I hope you never know. I forgave him before he ever laid a hand on me. He was as much a victim of that as I was, maybe more. I suffered the physical price, but he's cursed to carry the guilt for the rest of his life. It was Copernicus who beat me really, not Redge."

Forest touched Syrus' cheek. "Direct your hate to Copernicus. Forgive Redge."

Deep sorrow filled Syrus' eyes. "I'll try...I can't tell you what I went through when I lost you. He's the one who took you away."

"It could have been anyone. Redge was chosen to take me so Copernicus could rub salt in his wound. He's been through hell as well, just a different one."

He reached over and took her hands in his. "I'll try…to let go of my feelings." His eyes went oddly flat. "I have to ask you something difficult."

"What?"

"Before I faced Copernicus, I overheard him talking to Menjel about…about you and what he planned to do with you and the baby. Don't be afraid to answer me; I just have to know. Did he…" His voice almost failed him. "Did he sexually assault you?"

She reached up and touched his cheek. "No. He didn't."

He flinched and inhaled sharply. He blinked, his eyes going back to normal.

Forest told Syrus everything about her time with Copernicus. He told her everything else, leaving out the annihilation of the Fair. That could keep another day or two. He knew it would crush her, and she'd only just regained the strength to lift her head. When he got to the part of Redge showing up about an hour ago she cut him off.

"Syrus, go get him!"

"I'm not leaving your side."

"Then send someone after him. He might have the key to end this whole thing! We have to get him before Copernicus does."

"All right." He moved away from her and then hesitated, a look of indecision on his face. "I think I should talk to him myself. I need to look at him, take his measure. But I can't let him near you."

He strapped her sword around his waist.

"You look like you've become comfortable with my sword. Just don't forget it's *mine*."

He smirked. "So am I."

Syrus fished around in her jewelry until he found another spare End of the Bridge and went out into the garden. He approached Kindel who was standing near the gate.

"I'm going after Redge. Here." He handed Kindel the End of the Bridge.

"Go inside. If something happens in the few minutes I'm gone, break that open and take Forest out of here."

Kindel nodded and went into the house.

Syrus took a deep breath, wondering if he was doing the wrong thing, and pushed through the thick energy of the blood lock.

****

Redge and Journey walked away at a slow steady pace. She didn't press him for anything. He'd talk when he was ready. He seemed numb, but then he stopped walking, his shoulders shaking with tears. She reached for him, but he fell on his hands and knees. She knelt down next to him.

"Redge?"

"They got her out..." His voice broke around his emotion.

"What?"

"Forest. They got her out. Kindel said, she wasn't a captive of Copernicus anymore. They got her out! I almost killed her, he forced me to beat my friend almost to death. My *pregnant* friend!" He cried quietly for a moment. "I almost cost my best friend his mate and his child. I was sure they were lost to him. But they got her out! I ...I don't even have the words, Journey...I'm so relieved."

118

She held him. "You know you don't need words with me. I see what you're feeling. I'm glad you're happy."

He sighed and wiped at his eyes, getting back to his feet.

"So, how hard was it to defy the order not to contact people from your past?"

He frowned. "I don't know. I was so desperate I wasn't really paying attention."

"I think we should try it again. You had one more order, not to tell anyone where Forest was."

"Yes. That's right."

"I'm not going to sing for you this time. I want to see if you can do it without my help. Tell me where Forest is."

Redge opened his mouth to speak, but his slave mark woke up and tore into him. She watched him closely as he strained.

"Okay, stop. I have another idea. I'm impervious to the power of Regian marks, slave, or lover. I think when you broke through before, part of it was that I was singing, but maybe some of it was that you had recently bit me while we were intimate. It might have been helped by my blood in your system."

"How do you know you're impervious to marks?"

She rolled her eyes. "I remember when you tried to mark me. You thought I wouldn't know what you were doing."

Redge blushed at the memory. "I was a stupid boy. It was wrong of me on a few levels to try to mark you without your permission."

She laughed lightly. "You were just a little overeager to make sure I was all yours."

"I'm sorry."

She waved his apology away with her hand. "It doesn't matter now. Just bite me."

He drew her close and kissed her neck once before sinking his teeth through her skin. He took one small drink and pulled back. She waited a beat after he swallowed.

"Tell me where Forest is."

He grimaced in pain, sweat surfacing on his forehead. "She…uh…" He closed his eyes. "Ship."

"Ship? A ship where?"

He shook his head and rubbed his hand over the slave mark, letting out his breath heavily like he'd just been running a great distance.

"That worked," she said.

"Sort of."

"I have another idea. Can I have your knife?"

He looked at her dubiously but handed her the knife he kept in his boot.

"Take your shirt off," she ordered.

He raised one eyebrow and smirked but obeyed. "What are you doing?"

"I'm going to nullify your mark with my blood."

"Wait! You mean you're going to make me your slave instead?"

"I was going to try. Do you object?"

He looked thoughtfully bemused for a moment. "I must say it's a prospect I've never considered before. I find your idea oddly arousing… On the other hand, I think I'd have to turn over my man card if my woman has literal and total control over me."

Journey leaned in and kissed his mouth. "I don't want control of you. I can't force my will on you even if I put a slave mark on you. It goes against my nature."

"Does it?" he teased.

She gave him a dirty look.

"You're so beautiful when you're angry."

"Oh, shut up," she huffed. "Are we doing this or not?"

"Go ahead. Hack me up so I can be your boy toy."

Journey ignored his last remark and cut along the line of his scar. The wound hissed with smoke and tried to pull back together. She held the blade in the wound to keep it open and ran her finger along the edge. Her blood ran down the blade and into his open flesh. More smoke rose from the wound. Redge clenched his teeth against the pain.

"I don't think this is going to work," he said. "I'm sure other people have tried this before to rid themselves of slavery."

Journey ran her finger along the blade again, but this time she sang as her blood flowed into his body. His mind went fuzzy as she pulled the blade out and his skin sealed back together. He touched the mark. It felt cool and tingly under his fingers. She handed his knife back.

"Now tell me where Forest is," she ordered again.

"On a stolen ship, in the dead middle of the Crystalline Sea. In a cell below deck." His words came out easily. "Ha!" he shouted triumphantly, grabbing her, and spinning her in a circle. "It worked!"

"Redge?" A stern voice sounded behind them. One he knew very well.

Redge turned and saw Syrus.

Syrus was keeping his distance, Forest's intimidating sword in his hand, wariness and warning radiating off him. He looked at Journey, his eyes narrowing.

"You have Forest back?" Redge asked. "She's safe?"

Syrus didn't reply. His face remained impassive, but he twitched his wrist. The red light inside the black glass blade glimmered threateningly. Redge stepped protectively in front of Journey.

Syrus looked closely at Journey again, his eyes locking on hers. There was a recognition in his gaze.

"You *are* a Storyteller," he said slowly. "I remember one such as you in the castle when I was a child. Redge told me about you...I thought Storytellers couldn't come back once they left."

"I risked a great deal. It's illegal. But I came back to warn the keeper of my heart that he is in danger."

"What danger is that? Can you see the future? Did you know what Copernicus would do to him?" Syrus asked her.

"My world has regular trade agreements with the wizards. They are planning to take over Regia, along with other worlds that suit them. That is the danger I speak of. They are coming, soon."

Syrus blinked at her as though she had spoken in a language he didn't comprehend and then looked back at Redge.

"I thought Forest was still a prisoner. I came to tell you where to find her," Redge said. "Journey has made it possible for me to break Copernicus' orders. I'm not his slave anymore. Please believe me. Please forgive me for hurting Forest."

Syrus let out a ragged breath. "What Forest and I have gone through is unspeakable."

"I'm sorry," Redge said again.

Journey stepped around Redge and took a step toward Syrus. "You two have a very close bond. Friends for many, many years. If you will let me, I can help you communicate with each other with a greater level of honesty."

"What do you mean?" Syrus asked.

"I've read what's in your heart. Let me help Redge to understand what you've been through by translating that to him with my gifts."

"I warn you, you can't overcome me with your stories," Syrus said harshly. "You can't disable me."

She gave him a small bow. "You're right. You're too powerful, mage, to be rendered weak with my influence. You have nothing to worry about. I don't know you. Regia is not my home. I have nothing against you or your mate. I couldn't hurt you if I wanted to. And Redge, formidable as he is, is not your match either."

Syrus looked at Redge, who raised his eyebrows and shrugged in a male gesture that meant *it's up to you*.

"Fine," Syrus said, sheathing the sword.

Journey stood in between them and began to hum. Her voice pulled it all out of them, and they both looked at the apparition hanging in the air. It showed them things they knew. Just memories of the two of them as young men, but Journey pushed Redge's feelings on Syrus and Syrus' feelings on Redge. So they both knew exactly how the other had felt in the moments she showed them. They both laughed at a particular foolhardy and happy time.

She had them right where she wanted them, where they needed to be, before experiencing the intense pain she was about to inflict on them both.

The vision morphed into the very recent past. She started with Syrus, transferring onto him, and showing him everything Redge had gone through and felt as he became a slave. His heart responded fiercely as he absorbed it all. His hatred for Copernicus grew a new layer at what he had done to his friend.

Both Redge and Journey stepped back from Syrus as his eyes flashed electric red, lightning snapping through the grey of his irises. On the tail end of experiencing what Redge had endured, Syrus also got a flash of how he felt about having Journey come back into his life. He was impressed at the complexity and breadth of this love, over time and distance, and especially because they were not destined life mates. What Redge felt for Journey was different than the bond of life mates, but it wasn't fair to say it wasn't almost as strong.

Journey felt sorry for Redge as it was now his turn. She wished she could spare him from feeling Syrus' pain because reading Syrus' heart had broken hers. It was necessary, she told herself. Redge stumbled back, clutching at his chest as it all went in: the fear, twice over, of losing Forest, having to listen to her heart as it died, losing the child along with her. Having his best friend be the betrayer who took her away. The nameless emotions he'd suffered as he got her back almost too late and what he had to do to save her life.

Journey ended it and stepped aside as the two men looked at each other.

Redge was winded, holding on to his chest, a string of curses came pouring out of him. "I knew it was bad, but hell…"

Syrus smiled, satisfaction all over him, at Redge having to feel it all. He extended his hand to Redge. Redge took it. Syrus jerked him forward into a rough, brotherly hug. They slapped each other a few times on the shoulders. It was over; they didn't need to talk about it again. Journey smiled to herself. *Boys*, she thought. They could whack each other a few times when they were feeling something and then be fine, the balance of friendship restored.

"Can I see Forest?" Redge asked. "I'd really like her to meet Journey."

"Not until Merhl comes back. She's under a serious amount of security, and your blood wasn't in the construction of it." Syrus turned his full attention onto Journey. "Thank you, for…helping us mend our friendship."

She smiled. "I'd say it was my pleasure, but I didn't really enjoy putting either of you in pain."

"So the wizards are coming?"

"Yes, I'm afraid so," she said.

Syrus shook his head and rubbed his temple. "Why can't I have one crisis at a time? I need Rahaxeris' help. But he's been kidnapped by Copernicus, and the rest of the *Rune-dy* are dead."

Redge's eyes rounded. Syrus returned his meaningful look and nodded. "What does Forest think we should do?"

"She's only just woken up from her ordeal. And she doesn't know everything yet. When she gets a little stronger, I'll tell her what's happening."

Redge crossed his arms and pursed his lips. "I'm going back to Halussis and wait for someone from the Aluka Circle to come and find me. I'm going back in, only this time I know what I'm up against, and my slave mark has no hold on me anymore. But no one else needs to know that."

"Do you want Journey to stay with us? We'll protect her."

"No, or at least not yet. I need her."

"Are you sure? She'd be welcome."

"That's kind, but she wants—"

"Excuse me! You see me don't you? I'm right here." Journey interrupted them. "Don't talk about me like I'm not here. Or that I don't have a say where I go or what I do."

125

Both Redge and Syrus looked shamefaced. "Sorry," they muttered in unison.

"What do you want to do?" Redge asked her.

"I go where you go. I'm not finished helping you, and you're my slave. Remember?"

Syrus raised his eyebrows in question at Redge. Redge smirked and shrugged his shoulders.

"Okay," Syrus said slowly. "Not my business... So, I guess this is goodbye for now."

They hugged again, and Syrus kissed Journey's hand.

"Keep him out of trouble, won't you?"

She laughed. "I was never able to before, but I'll try my best...When we finish off Copernicus, I need to share all I know about the wizards with Regia's leaders."

Syrus nodded and turned away from them, fading back into the darkness as he left.

Redge sighed and leaned over, his hands on his knees, still coming down from the emotional wave. Journey panicked as she saw the self-loathing come back into Redge. Guilt rushed on him hard in the aftermath of truly feeling what his friend had been through, and he was blaming himself again.

"Look at me," she whispered.

He straightened, facing her. She kissed his mouth softly and began to hum again. His eyes snapped open, looking into hers, but she continued, keeping her lips against his, a low note vibrating in her throat. She took something from her own heart and pushed it on to him.

His eyes dilated as she showed him her daily experiences, waiting for his messages. She made him feel what it meant to her. He closed his

126

eyes and pulled her tightly against him. He pressed back on her, forcing her mouth to open to his, silencing her song.

"It's impossible," he said.

"That's what I thought, too. But it happened anyway."

"I never thought you could hear me. I never really knew why I did that every day, only that I felt I had to."

"Will you continue?" she asked.

"What?"

"Hearing you in that way, in my head, right as I wake, has become as much a part of who I am as my eye color. Losing it would break my heart."

"But you're right next to me," he argued.

"Doesn't matter. I watched you do it two days ago. I was only twenty feet away, and still I heard your written words like a whisper… Please?"

His expression softened completely, and he smiled a little. "Okay. I promise I'll never stop."

****

When Syrus came back under the blood lock, Kindel was pacing the far end of the garden.

"Why are you out here?" he asked.

"Netriet came in early. She's inside with Forest. I just thought I'd stay till you got back."

"Thanks. I appreciate it. If you see Redge again, he's back on our side."

Kindel left as Syrus went into his house. Netriet's and Forest's voices traveled into the entryway. He walked to the bedroom and leaned against the open doorframe. Netriet sat next to Forest, and they talked companionably. His heart lifted a little. Forest was sitting up and moving her head more normally.

"Merick and I went to the Wood to see if Shi might be of any help in locating you. But she didn't answer us. The whole place was still and silent, as though she wasn't there at all. We waited and called out for a while, but nothing."

"That's really weird," Forest said. "I don't understand it."

Both women looked over at him suddenly as though they just became aware of his presence.

"Did you find Redge?" Forest asked.

"Yes. And everything is all right."

"What happened?"

Netriet got up. "I'm going to leave you two alone." She headed out, and they heard the front door close behind her.

Exhausted, Syrus flopped onto the bed next to Forest.

"What happened?" she asked again.

He sighed loudly, resigned to telling her everything. Damn he was tired.

Chapter Fourteen

Copernicus paced in the dim light of his unassuming hideout in the lower middle-class suburbs of Paradigm. Rahaxeris was curled on the floor in the corner. He looked like a large, sickly baby, incapable of doing anything on his own. Copernicus was torn when he looked at his father, so he made a point not to. He had to focus on the next strike. His ultimate success hinged on his next move. It must be flawless.

His faithful ones were doing their jobs, gathering the slaves in the shadows, but Shreve had not returned. It had been too long. Something ill had befallen him. Copernicus was sure of it. Shreve must be dead, grievously injured, or trapped. He needed Shreve. But he didn't have the time to go looking for him. Plus, looking for him might endanger his own life. He thought back to his fight with Syrus. He couldn't risk going head to head with the mage again, not without some other advantage at least.

He looked at the map of Halussis he'd laid out on the table, stylus in hand, ready to mark strategic points he needed to place his slaves. He took a deep breath, trying to calm the sudden swell of fury rising inside him. He had no more ogres left in his ranks, having lost them all in the first strike. His original plans for taking the Onyx Castle were heavily dependent on his ogres. He'd needed them to open various portals for his slaves to use. So it was left to him to open portals during the next strike, a job he would have passed to Shreve.

Copernicus fiddled with Forest's portal ring that dangled from a chain around his neck. If only he had a few more of these. Or a handful of regular Ends of the Bridges, then he wouldn't have to worry about anything else because everything else was falling right into place. How could he get his hands on what he needed? Who could acquire them for his captains?

Copernicus should have been able to create End of the Bridges using his ogre blood, but it was a skill he had never learned, since he wasn't raised as an ogre with a family to teach him. He wasn't any good at constructing weapons either, as most ogres were. The only thing he could really do with the part of him that was ogre was open portals.

The most skilled ogres lived in the Onyx Castle. How could he get someone in there to take what he needed? His muddy hazel eyes slid out of focus as he remembered forcing one particular person to tell him everything about them, and he had lived in the castle…Redge. Where was Redge?

He'd ordered him to stay in Halussis and to keep away from his other slaves.

Copernicus closed his eyes and lifted the order, replacing it with a new one.

****

Redge and Journey were back at the ruin, resting in each other's arms on the hard, bare slats of the bed. Their time there was almost over. They only had a few more minutes really, but Redge refused to waste the fleeting moment in anxious stress over what they were about to do and the terrible danger they were throwing themselves into.

He gazed into her magenta eyes, his heart holding firm and steady. This was the only moment he had. The soul of everything, the world, love, loss, joy, and pain shrank down into this moment. One last fragment of what they could have had all these years and what they might have in the future, if only fate would be kind to them. He ran his fingers over her satin skin, committing the sensation forever in his memory.

"It's odd, isn't it?" she asked quietly. "Being together."

"In some ways, it was in the beginning, too. You, strangely gorgeous creature, deciding you would be mine. When your origins were from another world, another universe. You came such a long way to love me."

She caressed his face and smiled. "You're still so arrogant after all this time. I didn't come here for you. I just stumbled over you and found myself in a snare."

"Snare?" he repeated, insulted.

"Yes, and quite the snare you were, too. But that was before. This time, I did come a very long way for you."

He kissed her, taking hold of the end of this peace. It was time now for him to go. He pulled away from her with a heavy heart.

"Remember the plan, Journey. I'll be back as soon as I am able to. Don't come looking for me, please. If I'm lucky, I'll be back here by tonight. If fighting breaks out, be careful. Use your gifts to protect yourself... Please."

"I've been reading your heart. I promise I won't put myself in unnecessary danger. I know what losing me would do to you. I don't want to hurt you like that. And I appreciate you not trying to shut me out of this, even though you want to lock me away somewhere safe. Your faith in me to help with this means a great deal."

He kissed her one last time. His whole body hurt as he let go.

"Read me again," he said.

She looked at his chest and read his heart. She smiled at him. "I know," she replied to the unspoken words. "I love you, too."

He left, walking swiftly toward the city. He forced himself to leave his heart back there with her and closed his mind to thoughts of her. Redge took a deep breath, going hard and icy. He knew where to go. His mind had to be sharp, his lies quick, and his eyes open. He would fix it. He would reverse it all.

He went straight to the city square and stopped dead center. Fear hung in the air like an invisible toxic fume. Vampires moved around as normal, going about their business. The calm was a veneer. Redge took it all in. The strain was there, in their eyes, the tightness of their shoulders, and their smiles were determined, not happy or relaxed. Everyone felt it, even if they didn't know it consciously. The actions of the people told him clearly there was something going on under the surface in Halussis.

He took off down a side street and into an alley. He ducked under a doorway he knew would lead him to some of the Aluka Circle. A narrow, dark stairway took him up to the shabby living space. He almost tripped over the legs of a young man. Redge looked down at the vampire. He was on the point of adulthood, but he cried silently like a child. He looked up at Redge, his eyes slightly glazed, and rubbed at his slave mark. Redge felt the solid rock of his resolve grow a layer of calcium. He would fix this.

He entered the unfurnished space. Copernicus' slaves paced around the edges like animals in cages while three believers, the vampires that followed willingly, talked in hushed tones. They looked up at him as he approached. He didn't know their names, but he had come in contact with them before. A look of recognition came into the tallest one's eyes, and he reached out and grabbed Redge by the collar.

"Where have you been?" he demanded. "You're a day late. Everyone else responded to their summons. King Copernicus has new orders for you."

Redge looked down, acting subservient. "I'm sorry. I was taken hostage by a band of werewolves. They're a part of a new uprising."

"What's this nonsense?" the believer snarled.

Redge looked up and met his gaze, assuming an expression of shock. "You mean you don't know about the werewolves?"

The believer narrowed his eyes and cleared his throat. "Of course I know! I know everything." He turned to the two other believers. "You guys knew about the werewolves, didn't you?"

The others nodded emphatically. Redge laughed inside but kept his face schooled. The idiots. Anything to not lose face.

The believer who had him by the collar let go. "How did you get loose?"

"There were only a few. I killed them easily. I *was* a royal soldier before I joined the Aluka Circle, you know."

The believer scowled, obviously trying to hide that he was impressed. "Well, Copernicus needs you to go to the castle and get as many End of the Bridges you can. Since all the ogres who joined the Circle are dead, we need them to get into the castle so Copernicus can take the throne."

"When is the strike?"

All three believers gazes turned intently on him.

"How do you not know when the strike is?"

Redge gambled these vampires had never had a slave mark before. "I know I got my orders, but I can't remember. I did get hit on the head when I was taken by that wolf party."

This seemed to placate them. "The strike is the day after tomorrow. So you don't have much time to do as your master bids."

Redge gave them a little bow. "I should have no problem. I'll be back by the next dawn at the latest."

"Fine, now get out of my sight, slave."

Redge left, anxious to get out of the dark, cramped space. His breath came out in a small whoosh as he stepped into the open air, his mind turning over what he'd just learned. Oh, he'd go to the castle all right. He just hoped he could get in without a major issue.

The massive double doors on the main entrance of the Onyx Castle were shut tight and looked like they had been recently repaired. Burn marks stretched like long bony fingers up the wood. Four security ogres stood impressively on the stairs leading to the doors, all holding large, menacing weapons.

He recognized all of the ogres and had been on friendly terms with them in the past. He smiled at them.

"Koff." Redge gave the ogre a nod. "I need to get in. I have urgent information for Zeren. There will be a new hit on Halussis in two days."

The ogre, Koff, moved forward and looked down at Redge. "You've been blacklisted. I'm not supposed to trust you."

Redge pulled his collar down and showed the ogre his slave mark. "It's true. And the story is too long. I have to get inside." He held his hands up, his wrists together in front of him. "Arrest me."

The other ogres came up around Redge. Koff took a set of manacles from his belt and locked them around Redge's wrists.

"He wants in," Koff said. "Take him in."

Evidence of the recent fighting was all over the walls, just like it had been on the front doors. But as far as he could see, the castle hadn't suffered any damage beyond the cosmetic. Security was at an all-time high. Every guard was alert and carrying scary new weapons.

"I need to see Zeren. It's important."

The ogres behind him said nothing.

"Come on! I turned myself in. I've been undercover with the insurgents. I have intelligence. Plus, I used to outrank both of you by more than a fair amount. Give me something."

The long hall stretching out before him was empty. Then Zeren stepped out from a doorway. Redge had never been so relieved to see the former king in his life.

"Redge? What's going on here?" Zeren asked, looking down at his bound hands. "Syrus said you were lost to us."

"I talked with Syrus just last night. Apparently you didn't get the memo."

Zeren stepped closer to Redge and looked at the side of his neck. Redge turned his head so he could see the slave mark better. "It has no hold on me. I don't answer to Copernicus anymore."

"Slave marks don't lose their holds unless the master is dead," Zeren said flatly.

"This mark has a new master. Look, it's a long story, one I'm willing to tell you, but there is something more pressing. The insurgents are gathering to make another hit. In two days, Copernicus plans to take Halussis, and more importantly, the castle. He doesn't know that I can exert my own will. He thinks I'm still his. He wanted me to come here and get as many Ends as I can so he can filter his slaves in."

Zeren frowned.

"Don't trust me. That's fine, but Syrus can confirm that I'm myself again. My loyalty is here. Lock me up until you're satisfied."

Zeren nodded at the ogres behind Redge. "I'm sorry…I just have to be sure."

"I get it, just don't take too long. This is our chance to turn all this around."

The ogres pushed Redge lightly. He knew where they wanted him to go. He'd been in the cells of the castle countless times, but this was the first time he'd been in one as a prisoner. He paced the small, confined space three times, then Zeren was back ordering that he be released.

"All right. What's our move?" Zeren asked.

"Copernicus wants Ends, let's give him Ends that don't work. He's going to have the full, or close to the full, number of his forces here in the city."

"Why don't we just give him Ends that are set to land in one particular place? Then we can be ready at that location."

Redge paced the floor, his mind working furiously. The answer sparked, kindled, and blazed. "No," he said slowly. "Let's give him what he wants. We'll turn the tables on him right here, inside the castle."

"How?" Zeren asked.

"He has no ogres in his ranks, and we have a secret weapon... A Storyteller."

Chapter Fifteen

Syrus was instantly angry as he came into the bedroom and saw Forest on her feet. He grabbed her by the hand as her legs shook under her weight and threatened to give out.

"What are you doing?" he demanded. "You're not strong enough. Get back in bed."

She collapsed against him and cried in frustration. "I hate this! I have things I need to do. I need to save my father. I need to check on Shi."

He picked her up and laid her back down on the bed. "You can do nothing in both of those cases. Shi has been dead thousands of years, and your father is with your enemy. Pushing yourself will only result in more death, our child's and possibly yours." He kissed her forehead. "Now be a good girl and rest."

She scowled and nodded reluctantly, too tired to argue. "I want him dead, so, so much. I want Copernicus dead more than I ever even wanted Leith dead."

Syrus placed his hands on her rounding stomach. "This rage isn't good for you, Forest. Focus on something else." He smiled. "Who do you think the baby will look like? You or me?"

She snorted, falling victim to his misdirection. "Rahaxeris probably... Are you wishing for a boy?"

"No. I don't care either way. Do you think you know the sex?"

She shook her head. "It seems really weird to think about it being a boy, just for the fact that a small male is living inside me." She shook her

137

head again placing her hands on top of Syrus'. "I hope they look like you. I hope they *are* like you."

"Maybe they will be the best of both of us."

"Or the worst." She smiled, but then her smile faded into her fear. "You seem so happy. Are you not concerned at all that the baby isn't healthy? That the poison…that it…" Her breathing accelerated, and her heart hammered as she thought about it.

"Look at me," he ordered. "Shit happens, you know that. And we've been through a lot of shit lately. But we're still here. We still have each other, and our child's heart is still beating. I did all I could to restore you to health. There's nothing else I can do now."

"But what if—"

"What if, what? What if the baby isn't healthy? Are you going to not love them, Forest?"

She looked down at her hands resting over his, tears sliding down her cheeks. "Of course I will love them. I love them now."

"Be peaceful, Forest. We walk this life together. And we'll handle whatever comes, together."

She smiled through her tears and looked into his eyes. "You're making me weak again, Sucker."

She tugged on his hands. He let her drag him to her. He sat on the bed and wrapped his arms around her. She sighed and leaned her back against his chest as he put his hand back on her stomach. It was a perfect circle, the three of them. His aura wrapped around and over her. The bridge between their hearts flared a strong, soothing warmth. She sent his heart the immortal love she felt for him. Syrus absorbed it and sent it right back to her. It was one of those times when what they felt couldn't be conveyed in words. Spoken language was utterly inadequate. The words too weak, and lacked the proper context, but their hearts knew how to communicate.

A knock rapped on the front door. The noise burst the bubble around them. Syrus kissed her lightly and went to answer it.

"Father." He nodded to Zeren as he opened the door. "Come in."

"I just wanted to keep you in the loop," Zeren said as he came into the living room and sat down. "We know when Copernicus will strike next."

"Hold on," Syrus said. "Forest needs to know what is going on, too."

He went into the bedroom and carried Forest out and set her on the couch next to Zeren. Zeren hugged her. He began telling them all that Redge had learned and what they planned to do.

****

Shi held Ler and wouldn't let go. She couldn't remember feeling so light. It was all gone, the hate and the bitterness. She'd worn those emotions for ten thousand years, and now nothing of them was left, just the memory of how terribly heavy they had really been.

"Forgive me, Shi," Ler said.

"I have. Finally. At last. Forever. I forgive you... Forgive me for holding out so long."

"I love you," he whispered. "My queen."

His lips caught hers and held them.

So long, so very, very long she had been denied peace and any happiness. And her life had been so short, with only a few snatches of joy.

"I want to stay with you, Shi...but ever since you came inside to be with me...there's a pull deep within me. It's getting stronger. I don't know how long I can fight it."

139

"No," she whimpered.

"It's not what I want. I just don't know what to do. Can you curse me into being trapped with you again?"

Even as he spoke, she felt traces of him grow thinner and insubstantial in her arms. She couldn't curse him. The curse had come from her hate, and she had none left. All she had now was love. Could her love prove stronger? What could she do with it to keep them together?

"It's not fair. We only had a few days while we were alive. I can't let you go now, Ler."

"Don't, Shi. Don't let go. Think of a way before it's too late."

She entwined with him and kissed him deeply, breathing her spirit into him until they were less of two parts and more of one. The boundaries of separate identities shimmered and blurred, mixing together. She pulled him into herself and drew from her nature of being a tree. She would freeze them. Her will would make them go dormant and hold them in stasis.

A smoke-like substance billowed up around them from her petrified, crystal roots. In silence, in stillness, their love lived, content to exist without movement or change.

The Heart responded to them. The flames changed color from a dark grey to muddy layers, like a deep bruise. The trees chimed a new tune. One of bittersweet pain and a whispered wish for redemption.

****

Journey had a very long day. She waited, worried and relived so many memories. Most of them had taken place right where she was now. Memories were all she had for company. She was amazed at how young and foolish she and Redge had been and how they had mishandled the situation and their relationship. But regardless of their idiocy and mistakes, their love had proved real. It was real then, it was real now.

She sat on the slats of the bedframe and watched the sky thread its deep-hued ribbons over her head. The beauty of the Regian sunset made her heart ache. She remembered the first time she'd ever seen it and how the wonder of it alone made her happy she had chosen to come to Regia.

She rubbed her hands over her arms against the chill of the approaching night. She desperately wanted Redge to be back. Not just because she missed him—she did, terribly—but if he was back then she could stop worrying about his safety.

The sound of footfalls had her holding her breath, hopeful it was Redge, afraid it wasn't.

"Journey?" His voice washed over her.

She ran to him and slammed into his chest. "I missed you. I'm so glad you're back."

He held onto her tightly. "We need to go. I have to take you to the castle. We're on tonight. If we go now, we can bathe and change before we begin infiltrating."

Journey looked down at her dirty dress. So much had been occupying her mind she hadn't thought about such mundane details like the state of her clothes.

She smiled. "Let's hurry."

He took her hand, and they charged off into the lengthening shadows.

As soon as they arrived at the Onyx Castle, she noticed a marked difference in Redge. He held his head a little higher and his shoulders a little straighter. She continued to watch him from the side of her eye, pleased at his obvious pride, as they came into the massive front hall and everyone there acknowledged him with respect. He nodded formally to everyone but didn't stop to talk, instead, ushered her down a few hallways and through a large wooden door.

"This is my room," he said, smiling broadly. "It has been my room for many years."

She walked into the *room* which was less of a sleeping chamber and more of a complete and comfortable living space. The furniture was stately and everything from the window coverings and bedding to the rug on the stone floor were in dark colors and very masculine.

"It's lovely."

His smile grew so big she was afraid it would crack his face. "I wanted to show you everything I've—"

She cut him off. "I'm very proud of you."

He gathered her against his chest and kissed her deeply. "It's because of you."

"What is?" she asked.

"All of it. Everything I've done is because of you, and it's because of you I have it back."

She looked out of the window at the falling night, her mind returning to the task they had ahead of them. "We don't have much time. Where can I bathe?"

"Right through there." He pointed to a small door on the far wall.

She opened the door and gasped in delight as she was enveloped in warm, fragrant steam. She floated into the bathroom and began pulling at her clothes, anxious to get into the inviting bath that was already full of warm water. She turned and looked at Redge standing in the doorway. He took a step toward her then halted and shook his head.

"No," he scolded himself. "No time."

She smiled. "Close the door."

He waited for her. Then tried to take his mind off her in his bath by laying out the weapons he thought best for his task. Stealth was the game tonight. Small blades only. She came out after a few minutes, wrapped in a towel.

"Do you have something else for me to wear?"

He gestured to the bed where he'd laid out a plain black dress and hooded cloak for her. She stood at the side of the bed and picked up the dress. She raised one eyebrow at him. Dark heat surged into his eyes, and he came at her, only to stop short as he had a few minutes ago.

"No," he scolded himself again in the same kind of tone a parent uses on a small child. "No time."

He left her to get dressed, grabbing a pair of clean pants on his way to get washed up. When he came back into the room, hair dripping down his bare chest, he found her dressed and holding a handful of his clothes. He eyed the clothes and scowled.

"Really? You picked what you want me to wear? Is that where we are?"

"Hey, you picked my clothes." She rubbed her hand on the black fabric over her hip.

"Fine," he said in a more irritated tone than he felt as he reached for the shirt she held.

She shook her head. "No. I'm going to dress you."

He looked at her disbelievingly. She wasn't kidding. "Are you trying to emasculate me?"

She ran her hand up his chest, over the side of his neck, and fisted her hand in his hair before pressing her lips to his. "Just shut up and trust me," she whispered.

143

"Is that an order to your slave?"

"You bet it is."

She circled him. Her hand touched the top of his then skimmed up his forearm to his shoulder and played so lightly across his back, shivers rolled over him. He exhaled very slowly and closed his eyes. The fabric tormented his already sensitive nerve endings as she slid the sleeves up his arms. She kissed his mouth feathery-light as she laced the front of his shirt closed. Then she moved on to the light armor he had intended to wear.

She stopped being as gentle as she tightened the straps of his vambraces, causing him to hiss through his clenched teeth. It was like some terribly effective backward seduction.

"You are in *serious* trouble when this is over tonight," he threatened her.

"I hope so…I think it's time to go now."

He looked out the window and nodded. He grabbed up the last knife she hadn't slid into his belt or boots. It was a very slim, short blade. He pulled her close and pushed the knife into the top of her braided hair like a comb. She frowned and touched the top of the handle.

"I can't. I've never carried a weapon of any kind. I don't think I could inflict pain even if I needed to." She made to pull it out.

He stopped her hand. "Please, just humor me." He cupped her face in his hands, a worried look creasing his brow.

"What?" she asked.

"We don't have to do this. I mean, I'm sure it will work. It worked on me. Why do we have to test it?"

"It only sort-of worked on you. Plus, you and I are connected to each other. It's not exactly anything I've ever done before. I need to test

144

it. You said our success against Copernicus rests on this. If it doesn't work the way we think it will, you've got to form a whole new strategy. There are too many unknown variables."

"All right," he conceded. "I hate unknown variables."

She smiled. "Everything in life is full of them."

He kissed her roughly. "Not everything. Not us."

She frowned but didn't contradict him with words.

They slipped out into the night, hooded, and hand in hand. He led her silently through the empty back streets of Halussis. He was amazed at her trust. When they had first come up with this plan, he'd never thought she would really go through with it. Redge looked at her. Journey's face was shadowed, but the moonlight fell on her beautiful full mouth and her chin. She wasn't even holding her jaw tight. He hadn't earned this level of trust. Why did she give it?

He held his finger to his lips as they rounded the corner and stopped near the doorway that led to the gathering place of Copernicus' slaves that he'd visited just that morning.

"Stay back until I've made it safe. If something goes wrong, bow down and blend in with the slaves. Act like one of them until you can get out." His voice was barely audible, even right next to her ear.

Redge tied a black scarf around the lower half of his face and pulled his hood down farther. Only his eyes were visible. He crossed under the threshold and melded into the shadows on the stairway. He slunk silently to the upper room and held still in a dark corner. Most of the slaves slept on the bare floor, while some sat and rocked slowly. The moonlight shone through the single window and onto the heads of two of the believers who talked quietly to themselves. Redge scanned through the dark space, looking for the third. He couldn't see him anywhere.

He darted through the shadows and came up right behind one of the believers. One of his knives sank deep into the vampire's back, just under the ribs. The knife in his other hand bit handle-deep into the side of his neck. Blood sprayed across the other vampire as Redge pulled his knives back out. The other believer stumbled backward, trying to get away, and was dead before he hit the ground, one knife in his heart, the other in his ear.

Those asleep roused in confusion. In a moment, everyone was on their feet. A warm golden light stretched through the space. Everyone turned. Journey stood in the doorway, a flickering orb in her hands. They moved aside for her, and she met Redge in the middle of the room.

"Where is the other believer?" Redge demanded.

"He left to report to Copernicus."

"Listen to me," he said, adding an edge of authority to his voice "I used to be one of you, but now my slave mark has no control over me because of her. This is Journey. She is a Storyteller. She can help you regain control of your own will… Maybe you came to Copernicus willingly, maybe you were forced. I don't care. Who among you would free yourselves and help stop all of this?"

Every person raised their hands and said, "I," or "I would."

"Okay. Open your minds and your hearts to her and listen well."

Journey tossed the light orb into the air. It hit the ceiling and broke apart, scattering glittering light particles that winked and floated like dust motes through the air. One low slow note sounded in her throat, and she turned in a full circle. Everyone's mind relaxed open to her into the sleepy semi-conscious state she used as her medium to paint with. She raised her voice a few octaves and turned in another circle, looking into each heart.

A single golden thread pulsed out from every chest and hovered lazily in the air over Journey's head. She reached up and gathered them in her hands, beginning to lace them together. She used only the best attributes in each person: courage, honesty, kindness, goodness, and love. However small the seeds might be, she fed them, and they began to grow. Their hearts turned to soft clay in her hands, and she deftly began to re-shape them. She didn't turn them into anything they weren't, just what they were always capable of becoming. She sloughed off the hard edges placed there by bitterness, disappointments, and loss.

They all looked up as the story began. Her hum became a real song, and the ghostly tapestry manifested in the room. Every person saw themselves, like a player on a stage. She sang them a story of a wondrous time of peace and prosperity coming to Regia and how they could all be a part of it, if only they would set aside their prejudices and fight together for an ideal.

The story took time, each person profoundly and intimately affected.

Journey exhaled as she finished. It was the best and hardest work she had ever done, and now she was exhausted.

Everyone looked around in wonder as they came back to full lucidity. A few rubbed at their slave marks.

"Did it work?" someone asked. "Are we free?"

"I don't feel any different. My mark is still there."

"What is going on here?!" an angry voice yelled from the doorway.

Everyone turned. The last believer had come back. Before he could do more than yell, the slaves rushed on him and swallowed him up like a tidal wave. Redge pushed forward through the mob. They backed away from him as he looked at the believer, stomped to death on the floor. He checked to make sure he was really dead and then looked back to Journey.

"I guess it worked," he said with a broad smile.

"I fear," Journey spoke up. "The effects are temporary."

"Let's leave while we have the chance!" someone else said.

"No!" Redge said harshly. "You'll ruin your chance at full freedom. Stay together. Act as though nothing has happened, and you'll get your chance to free yourselves permanently. Don't try to rebel until you see her again." He gestured to Journey. "When you see her again, then your time will have come. Remember my words. Remember her song."

He picked up the body and carried it over his shoulder. Journey followed him. He didn't make any attempt to hide the body; he left it in the next alley. They went back to the castle.

****

This is where I want to stay, Journey thought, as she rested her head on his shoulder. He'd dozed off, sitting with his back against the bed's headboard, one arm draped around her. She stared at his relaxed profile, noting the wear and tear of years, and again, she grieved the loss of them. There was so much going on that they hadn't had the time, or perhaps the presence of mind, to talk about the things she felt they needed to.

He was a guy, and he was acting like one, she mused. He didn't think there was anything to deal with or overcome between them. They had love and passion and what else could there be? They were together, and that was that to him. He would ask her to stay with him. She knew that; it wasn't a question. But could she? Even if she could, would Regia's leaders let her? Would they give her citizenship? Perhaps if she proved useful enough. Guilt began to poke at her. Just one more day to get through. If they could kill Copernicus, then she could focus on helping Regia as a whole, form a plan to stop the annihilation that was coming from the wizards.

Not that she had the answer. She wished desperately that she did, but all she had was the bad news. All she could offer them was knowledge, and perhaps a chance.

Her heart began to ache. She closed her eyes and focused on healing herself. The moisture on her cheeks alerted her. One tear fell on his chest, rousing him from sleep. He pulled her closer and kissed her temple.

"Why are you crying?" he asked softly.

She wiped the tears away with the back of her hand. "I'm overwhelmed. I need to focus on feeling one thing at a time. There's just so much…"

"I know. I promise you, when all this is over, we'll go away together for a while. Just you and me."

She sighed. "I fear it's going to be a long time before you can fulfill that promise, if you can at all."

"Hey, it's going to be all right. I know our plan will work. We proved it tonight."

"Yes, I believe it will work. But what about after? The future of Regia is shaky."

"We'll figure it out. I know we will. I can't believe my world is about to die, I won't believe it," he said fiercely.

She laced her fingers through his. "I understand your feelings. But if there is no hope, will you leave Regia with me?"

He looked at the far wall, his deep-water eyes slipping, unfocused. He was quiet for a moment. She waited for his reply with her heart in her throat. Then he closed his eyes and let out a ragged breath.

"And what of my friends? Will they be welcomed in your world, too?"

"I don't know." The truth brought her sorrow. "When, *if* I go back, I'll have no standing, no status, and no livelihood. I will be convicted and punished for breaking the law…for coming back here. I'm pretty sure I could work a deal for you, but beyond that, I wouldn't have the influence. I'm sorry."

He was quiet again for a little while.

"I love you, Journey. And I would follow you anywhere, but I don't know if I could abandon my friends, my world, to save myself. How could I leave in the moment I might be needed the most?" He leaned forward and put his head in his hands. "If... If we can stop this from happening, will you stay here with me?"

"I," she said slowly, "I would like to." He looked back at her, and she grimaced. "I'm sorry. That was less than the answer I know you wanted. I just don't want to lie to you."

"You're going to leave me again? You always were?"

"No! I didn't have a plan when I came here, except I had to warn you. I had to try to save you. I didn't have any idea that you would feel anything for me anymore. I didn't know if you had found love with someone else, or if you had found your destined life mate. Perhaps you had four kids, I didn't know anything!" her voice rose. "I risked so much!"

"What else do you want from me, Journey? Beyond what I have already given you? I killed my own father to save your life, and I lost you because of it. I gave you my soul, and you took it with you. I have nothing to offer anyone else. All of me lives in you. It always did. I was faithful to you, when all I had was a phantom that haunted my dreams at night... Then you came back here, and you showed me your truth that night...the night I thought I was dreaming, but you were there. If you wanted to or not, you let go of control and showed me what was inside you. Our love is not in question." His angry expression softened, and he smiled a little bemusedly. "I'm your slave, remember?"

She snorted and then shook her head. "I'm sorry. Don't be angry with me. I'm afraid."

"Afraid of what? War?"

"No," she whispered. "I'm afraid of losing you again. Afraid I was always doomed to lose you in the end."

"This has no end. I told you, you hold my soul. When I die, if it's tomorrow or the next day, or a thousand years, I will be with you, and so will my love."

Chapter Sixteen

Copernicus rolled Forest's portal ring between his thumb and index finger, his mind swirling. One more day. Just one more, and he could leave behind all of this mediocrity. He would be the king, and he would make sure no one could stand against him. He'd already disposed of the *Rune-dy,* and they had been his greatest threat inside Regia. But he would make sure the wizards, the greedy, evil wizards would not breach the wall he would build around the world. He was the savior.

Rahaxeris wheezed from the corner. Copernicus looked over at him. He was getting worse. He would die soon. A sharp pain struck him in the heart. It wasn't what he wanted. He wanted his father's love and support, but he didn't know how to get it. And since he didn't have Rahaxeris' love, he had no choice but to leave him hobbled.

Forest. He still had Forest. He comforted himself with that thought. Grasping power had robbed him of Shreve, and his fantasy of a relationship with his father was gone, but he had Forest… and her baby. They were all mixed and spliced. Quite the family they would be.

He closed his eyes as he waited for the next round of reports to come in from his believers and for Redge to bring him his victory insurance. He thought about Forest while he waited. His sister, his queen. He'd make her pay for the pain her mate had dealt him, but then, when she'd felt the sting enough, he'd forgive her. He ground his teeth together as he thought about the way she'd react when he finally did kill Syrus. She'd cry, no doubt. He would punish her for that, too. Then everything would be okay.

He opened his eyes and glared at the follower, who had just come in and bowed before him. "King Copernicus," he said.

"Is everyone ready?"

"Yes. The slaves are all assembled at every location and waiting. When will we have our portals?"

"Right now," Redge said, coming into the room. He bowed his head and held out a handful of silvery balls on chains and placed them on the middle of the map laid out on the table. "It was not an easy task. I got as many as I could."

Copernicus stood and counted the balls. "Good. There are enough." He moved closer to Redge and looked down at him, calculating. With one finger, he pushed down on Redge's slave mark.

Redge winced, and sweat beaded on his forehead.

"I'm ordering you to tell me the truth. Do you know what happened to Shreve?"

"No, my lord."

Copernicus sighed and went back to his chair. "Fine…fine. Take those," he said to the believer, pointing at the pile of Ends. "Make sure every location has one."

"Yes, my king."

Copernicus turned his full attention on Redge as the believer left. "What did you see in the castle? New security? Anything I should be aware of that might trip us up tomorrow?"

"There are extra ogres at the entrances, but nothing beyond that."

"You will stay here with me, now. You can replace Shreve as my right hand." He smiled then. "Have you been having nightmares about Forest?"

"Yes, my lord."

His smile broadened. "Good. I think I may have been wrong before when I said you would never see her again in this life. I hadn't anticipated losing Shreve then…But then again, I'm not sure I'll keep you alive after tomorrow. We'll see. I have to admit I prefer real allegiance over the obedience of slaves."

Rahaxeris groaned from the corner. "Forest is dead. You killed her."

Copernicus rolled his eyes. "Take him outside," he ordered Redge. "See if the sunlight might help him feel better. I would like him to live a few more days at least, so I can show everyone how I conquered the *Rune-dy*."

"Yes, my lord."

Redge leaned down, hooked his hands under Rahaxeris' arms, and lifted him up. The elf felt like an empty rubber bag. He couldn't walk, let alone stand, so Redge picked him up and carried him outside. Rahaxeris' physical state was disgusting, but Redge still preferred his society to Copernicus'. A tiny enclosed yard jutted off the back side of the house. Broken stone work, overgrown weeds, and a stone bench made up the whole yard. He set Rahaxeris on the bench and sat next to him, letting the elf rest his head against his shoulder.

"Who are you?" Rahaxeris' voice came out in a wet hiss.

"A friend of Forest's," he whispered. "We've met at Fortress. I used to work for her, remember?"

Rahaxeris lifted his head a fraction and tried to focus his crusted eyes on Redge's face. He blinked a few times. "Redge?"

"That's right."

His head rolled back down, his chin against his chest. "Forest is dead…" He moaned. "My daughter is dead."

Redge looked around carefully before putting his mouth right at Rahaxeris' ear and whispering, "She lives. She escaped. I've seen Syrus. He has her."

Rahaxeris lifted his head slightly, his eyes clearing a little, and his gaze pushed deep into Redge's, probing and searching. Then he closed his eyes and took a few labored breaths. "You speak the truth… Thank you."

"What's wrong with you?"

He tilted his head to the side and tapped the cuff on his neck with a shaking, emaciated finger. "Could you remove it?"

Redge frowned. "If I do, will you be yourself again? Can you end this?"

"I don't think I will be myself immediately. It has been on too long. I will need some time to strengthen."

"That's time we don't have."

"Pull out the pin in the hinge. I'll leave the cuff on. Copernicus won't notice."

Redge looked around again before pulling the pin in one swift move. He leaned over and buried it in the dirt under the bench, making sure the ground looked undisturbed before he straightened back up. Rahaxeris took a deeper breath, and he seemed to re-inflate a bit.

"Act sick," Redge said.

"I will, don't worry." His voice was still weak, but it was stronger already. He touched Redge's throat with his index finger. A buzzing covered his skin where Rahaxeris touched him. "Now, no one can hear you but me. Tell me the plan."

****

Zeren unrolled the note Ithiel brought from Forest and Syrus. He read it carefully twice, considering their advice on the prep for Copernicus and his slave army. Zeren was grateful for Forest's new insight on the enemy's personality. Almost everything was ready in the

155

castle, as ready as it could be. Every ogre had been briefed and given their assignments. They followed Zeren's orders without question, as though he was still the king.

Zeren handed the letter to Ithiel. "See what you think," he said, prompting the master to read the letter as well.

He did.

"I think we should do as she says. I think we should pair as many ogres as we can with a Kata master. Just as a double measure. My men have been practicing neutralizing moves, so they won't accidentally kill any of the slaves… Despite everything, I'm sure there will be a loss of life on both sides. But we will keep it minimal."

"All right. Let's do as Forest says. I moved the thrones from the throne room months ago and put them in a closet. I'll have a few ogres get them and bring them back in." Zeren scratched his chin. "Forest said it should be theatrical. I know where all the tapestries, rugs, and fancy crap Christiana used to have in there went." Zeren sighed and gave Ithiel an apologetic look. "Well, let's get this over with. Want to be the head decorator?"

Ithiel wrinkled his nose as though he smelled something foul. "Aren't there any women that still live in this place?"

"Not really. The castle is more of a place of community service now. All the flouncy bunnies have scampered off, not wanting to get their hands dirty with real work. Come on, I remember how it looked. We'll get it close enough."

Ithiel followed Zeren. "So happy I didn't have to guard Forest today so I could be here for this," he said sarcastically.

****

Journey left the castle not long after Redge went to take the Ends to Copernicus. She left Halussis on the empty back ways, wearing her hooded cloak. She went back to the ruin. Not because she was supposed

156

to, but she felt compelled to be alone. She stood in the empty space and closed her eyes. Her life had begun here. The life that truly was hers, her choice. All that time ago, she had decided to make her home in Regia. She'd never been given the chance to tell Redge that. She'd meant to the night she ended up running back home.

Her memories rushed on her, images flashed and blurred into a painful collage. If only she could go back and talk to her younger self. She'd tell herself not to fall for him. She'd tell herself not to come to Regia at all. It didn't matter now because she had and she did.

Providing they survived tomorrow, and a solution to hold back the wizards was reached, what kind of a future did she and Redge have?

She shook herself. Questions didn't matter. Their relationship wasn't conventional, so what? It wasn't like they hadn't had the chance to move on. But neither of them had. She thought about the nature of love. With most, the love between two people was like a living machine. But with her and Redge, their love was like a statue, unmoving, unchanged, and stuck perhaps. It existed, and it wouldn't change. In ways that was comforting, and others, a sorrow. Their love wouldn't create a family. Journey longed to be a mother, but their DNA was too different to mix and create new life. She would never bear him children. He knew it as well as she did.

Journey sighed and released the past back into her depths. There were things *she* wanted and just for the moment she allowed herself to want them. She looked around. Why was she here? What had compelled her to come to this tomb of pain? She walked to the open hole of a window and grabbed a stone from the top. It came free in her hand. The ones next to it fell to the ground. She smiled to herself. Now she knew why.

She walked outside the ruin, took off her cloak, and laid it across a stump. She found a thick, fallen branch on the ground and rammed it into a crack in the wall with all of her might. The crack lengthened. She hit it again and then jumped backward as the whole wall began to crumble, then it caved and fell. Dirt flew up into a cloud, and the crashing sound hurt her ears. The wall now lay in a huge pile of stones and broken mortar. A strange kind of laugh bubbled up her throat. She let it loose.

Journey rammed each wall in turn until the whole house was no more. Just a mound of rocks around the tree that had grown in the center, through the roof. She dropped her battering ram from her blistered hands, put her cloak back on, and headed back to the Onyx Castle. Sweaty, dirty, and elated. She'd broken the skeleton hand of the past and its hold on her. She would live right now, in this moment, however short it may be. If the end was upon them, she would wring out every last drop and savor slowly.

She wanted Redge back, but she had no choice but to wait. She banked the fire inside her and let it smolder. She wouldn't put it out. She'd let it build pressure until he came back to her.

Chapter Seventeen

Forest tried to sleep. She tried *really* hard to sleep. It just wasn't happening. Her mind wouldn't let go of the horrible *what ifs* that could and would come with the dawn. The beast was at the gate, ready to charge. And she had to be still, robbed of her power to fight. Syrus was right next to her, his chest pressed against her back, his arm wrapped over her. If he wasn't asleep, he was doing a good job of faking it. His steady breathing brushed over her shoulder again and again.

A sharp wrenching twisted in her abdomen, and she gasped in pain. As soon as the pain started, it stopped. Then it struck again. It felt like her body was stretching outward. She grabbed Syrus' arm and pulled his hand to her belly, pressing his palm flat against her skin, just under her navel. He roused then, his electric power sliding from his hand and entwining with the snapping current inside the baby. The pain eased. It was like a strange form of communication between Syrus and the baby, a recognition or understanding.

"You okay?" he asked sleepily.

"You make the pain better. The baby responds to your touch…I guess we don't need a paternity test," she teased.

"What test?" He sat up, rubbing his eyes.

She laughed gently. "To prove who the father is. You know, Earth stuff."

He sighed and got up from the bed, too tired or preoccupied to respond to her jest. He looked out the window at the dark sky. "I'm glad your sense of humor is back," he said flatly.

"I'm sorry I woke you. You still seem tired. Come back to bed. You need your strength. You have to fight for the both of us tomorrow."

"No, I don't." He lay back down in the same position, placing his hand on her stomach. "I'm staying here with you. But I do need my strength to protect you *and* so I don't get too angry with you when you make stupid jokes."

"Sorry. I just wanted to hear you laugh."

He kissed the back of her head. "Go to sleep. Your snore always makes me laugh."

"I don't snore!"

He did laugh then. "Wanna bet?"

The sound of his chuckle made her feel worlds better, even if it was at her expense. For one second she was able to pretend everything was good and fine.

"Maybe we should sleep in different rooms so I don't keep you awake at night," she offered.

"Oh, no." He pulled her tighter against him. "Your snore is really quite cute. More of a little wheeze." His tone went all desperate ex-boyfriend. "Please, don't leave me to sleep all alone! I'd have to walk *all the way* across the house in the middle of the night to seduce you. I can't handle it!" he wailed.

She elbowed him in the ribs and laughed. "I like you."

"You *like* me?" he repeated.

"Yes. You're my mate, and I love and desire you, but I also like you. You're my favorite person."

"Hmm." His voice rumbled with pleasure. "Well, I *like* you, too."

She sighed and nestled down into his embrace and was finally able to slip into an uneasy sleep.

****

The night held long and tight like a breath trapped in the lungs. Merick held perfectly still under his cloak, trying to keep warm in the cold night. His ears stayed perfectly alert, but he closed his eyes. He hated being this close to where the Fair had been, but it was his turn to be on guard for Forest. He worked to keep the bitterness and desolation at losing his friends from eating him up completely. He never would have been able to manage by himself. But Netriet kept him warm. Her love softened the hardness on his heart and prevented it from turning to cold stone.

His breath came out in a puff of steam as the temperature dropped a bit more. He looked at the house and then looked away. He wouldn't ask Syrus for anything, not even a hot drink. He wouldn't ask, not because he thought he would be refused, but because he knew, better than anyone, what Syrus had just gone through, almost losing his mate and child. He didn't know what they were doing in there, and he wouldn't be the one who interrupted their solace just because he was cold.

Approaching footfalls had him springing to his feet. A silhouette moved through the depth of the blood lock and emerged in the garden. He relaxed before she was all the way through, recognizing Netriet's awesome curves and the familiar sway of her hips as she walked.

"What are you doing here?" he asked.

She smiled and held out a thermos, as if she had telepathically known what he wanted. He took it, wrapping his cold fingers around its warmth.

"It's coffee. We're out of tea."

"You're an angel. How did you know?"

She shrugged. "What's to know? You're out here in the cold. I would have wanted the same thing."

He sat back down. Holding one side of his cloak open, he beckoned her closer with a jerk of his head. She sat down next to him, and he wrapped the cloak around her, too.

"Have you decided if you're going to the castle to fight in the morning?" she asked.

"I think I'm too angry still. I doubt I could hold back the way Zeren is saying we have to because they are slaves. I know it's not their faults, or not completely. But my friends..." He ground his teeth together. "Apparently the only target I have for my rage is Copernicus, and there is no way I'm going to be able to get close to him. Everyone wants his blood. Everyone has a right."

She pressed a kiss on his neck. "Yes, even me. They were my friends, too...You know we are damn near close to unstoppable when we fight side by side. We could—"

"No. It's your shift in the morning, right?"

"Yeah."

"I'll stay here with you." His breath came out raggedly and puffed in the air again. She snuggled closer, warming him. "Let's talk about something else."

She smiled, a mischievous light coming into her eyes. "Forest being pregnant has got me thinking."

He groaned. "No way. No babies. I'm too old."

She snorted. "Well, I'm not... She told me they weren't trying. Sometimes life just happens, Merick."

He narrowed his eyes at her. "You're plotting. No more sex for you."

She laughed. "Uh huh. I really believe you mean that."

"With everything going on in the world, how can you even think about having a child right now?"

"Not right now. I just wanted to start a dialogue about it. That way when I really mean it, it won't blindside you. And now that you're all fussed and uncomfortable, I get the joy of dropping it into the conversation every so often just to see you squirm. You have to admit that—"

He turned her chin with his hand and caught her mouth with his. He patiently kissed her, the way he knew melted her bones and scattered her thoughts. She sighed into him. Then her eyes snapped open, and she pulled away.

"Why do you always do that?"

"Too much chatter, Netriet. It's the only guaranteed way I have to shut you up."

She gave him a dirty look that only lasted a second then turned hungry. "Kiss me like that again, Merick."

"You didn't say please."

She put her mouth on his ear and whispered in her most seductive voice, "Now."

He raised his eyebrows. "You're real trouble." He captured her mouth again, and for just a little while, they shut out the worry.

****

Rahaxeris' strength returned at a steady pace. He huddled in the dark corner on the floor, looking feeble, but feeble no longer. He still wasn't himself, and he didn't have the confidence to try anything. The loose cuff on his neck didn't cripple him now, but its contact with his skin still held him back in recovering fully.

Copernicus slept in short bursts, getting up now and then to pace around and talk to himself. Redge spent the night in a straight-backed chair by the table. He dozed off a few times, his head hanging down on his chest. Rahaxeris watched Redge. The slightest noise alerted him. He was more than grateful to him for everything he had done and was doing. If they both lived through the day, he would come up with a way to reward Redge.

The dawn was a mere hour away, and Rahaxeris turned his mind to the problem beyond that of the next few hours, onto the wizards and how he could possibly stop them. As soon as the faintest trace of color smeared the sky, Copernicus was up. He came out of his room, fully dressed and armored. An elaborate cape embroidered with gold hung from his shoulders.

Redge stood and bowed to him. Copernicus glanced at him but otherwise ignored him. He laid five swords on the table and considered each of them in turn. In the end, Copernicus chose the largest one, favoring intimidation over the sword that would have proved more efficient. He walked over to Rahaxeris and looked down at him.

"What do you think, Redge? Should we take him with us?"

"Definitely, my lord. It is a great show of your power and will frighten those opposed to you into submission."

Copernicus grunted in the back of his throat. "All right. He's your problem. You carry him. Choose a weapon. It's time to go."

Redge grabbed one of the swords off the table and strapped it around his waist. He lifted Rahaxeris up the same way he had the previous day.

Copernicus closed his eyes. "I'm sending out the order now. The castle will fall. I have no doubt. My entire force will be there. The numbers alone are too much for them to stand against, and they will be taken by surprise," he said, a terrible smile spreading over his mouth. "Many will die. My slaves will fight without honor." He called on his ogre DNA and opened a portal.

Redge's blood ran cold as he followed Copernicus into the black mouth of the portal. He was bringing the danger to his home, his friends, and to his love.

Chapter Eighteen

They were coming. Journey could feel it like a buzz in between her shoulder blades. She looked at herself in the mirror and raised her eyebrows. She'd never worn armor or carried a sword. She looked like a Valkyrie, but she was sure she didn't feel like one. *Please...Please be kind*, she begged fate. She left Redge's room and joined the others. She could see it on their faces; she didn't need to read their hearts. They felt the enemy coming, too.

Zeren came up to her. "Are you ready?"

She nodded quickly.

"Follow me to the throne room."

She followed him, her throat going dry.

He ushered her over to the side of the ornate, overdone space, where the wall stopped and opened around the side to a hidden door. He opened it, and she followed him into the plain room. It was empty except for racks and racks of weapons. It was an adequate space for her to play her part.

"Stay hidden until the right time," Zeren ordered. "Everything will come to you."

Again she nodded, unable to speak.

A loud crash sounded overhead from the floor above them, followed by yelling and clanging metal. The first wave had arrived. Zeren's eyes burned brightly, and he drew his sword.

"Stay hidden," he said again and left her alone.

Journey pressed her back against the wall behind her and wrapped her arms around herself, her hands digging in and holding tight. Her bottom lip trembled as the sounds of fighting and death grew louder and echoed in her ears. Her mind clung to Redge. *Please survive.*

Portals opened all over the Onyx Castle, flooding every level with vampires, werewolves, elves, and shape-shifter slaves. They charged ahead ruthlessly, unable to give in to any fear or feel any remorse. They operated under Copernicus' orders to use any and all dishonorable means without holding back.

The royal soldiers fighting against the insurgents were ordered to preserve life as much as possible, but that was a difficult task, especially against the wolves, who all fought in deadly beast form, and the elves were all invisible. The shifters weren't built for fighting like the others and went down easier. After a few moments, those fighting against the insurgents knew what they were up against.

Half of the castle's ogres used their nasty weapons to hack through the ocean of attackers. They too worked to preserve life, only doing as much damage as necessary to disable and neutralize. In spite of that, bodies hit the floor. Many bodies on both sides.

The invisible elves were dealing the hardest blow to the royal soldiers. Their swords and knives flashed in the air, giving them away. But there was so much crashing metal that mostly the elves' blades just mixed into the chaos. Dispersed through the crowd, the elves only became more noticeable as blood began to cover them.

The Kata masters were able to move faster than anyone else. They targeted the invisible elves, plucking their weapons from their hands, but after a moment, that action proved worse as the elves attacked the soldiers from behind. Having nothing but their hands, the elves took to sneaking behind their opponents and snapping their necks.

The ogres not fighting came behind the action, gathering up the disarmed and wounded, opening portals and sending them straight to where Journey waited.

167

She jumped as the first bloodied and disoriented group landed in a heap in front of her. She lifted her voice immediately in song, having no time to waste to read these people. They were under killing orders and would end her without hesitation. She sang faster and more forcefully than she ever had, throwing images into the air above the crowd.

They all listened and watched as she freed them temporarily from the hold of their orders. Most had broken hearts at what they had just been forced to do and many began to weep. She had to re-direct their emotions. Remorse would have to wait. There was no time for it now.

They gazed on her like she was an angel, beyond touching, and divine.

"You have to change sides," she said. "Prepare to fight for your freedom."

As soon as they got to their feet and began to choose new weapons from the racks, another group fell into the room, and she had to repeat the process all over again.

The next bunch took less time as adrenaline pushed her. These were also less wounded. As soon as they had a small measure of self-control back, they turned on one of the group and killed him with their bare hands, tearing his limbs from his body. Journey realized he must have been another believer and not a slave. A few of them spit on his body as they joined the others in choosing new weapons.

The insurgents' numbers were taken down by death or Journey's conversion. Zeren fought with his men, but the time began to look right for their next action as Copernicus had yet to be spotted. He shouted over the noise for half of his men to pull back. They understood, knowing this order would be coming. They pulled back and funneled down to the bowels of the castle and waited. The rest continued to fight the unconverted.

***

Copernicus' portal brought him into the center of the throne room. Redge stood beside him, Rahaxeris hanging from his arm, limp like a dead body. He filled his lungs to their full extent and let loose a roar so loud it halted the whole castle. Copernicus held his massive hands up in front of him, his fingers splayed. An eerie blue light glowed under his fingernails, and he moved his hands through the air, forming some kind of otherworldly barrier over himself and the throne. Redge panicked as he realized he and Rahaxeris were caught under it with him.

"The throne is mine! The Onyx Castle is mine! *Regia* is mine! Stop fighting! You've lost. I am King! Bow to me!"

All of the slaves still fighting threw down their arms and knelt. The soldiers stopped attacking, unsure what to do and unwilling to kill the unarmed people in front of them.

"Put down your weapons!" Copernicus bellowed. "No one else needs to die. If you bow to me now, I will not unleash the rest of my forces, ready and waiting, into the public to kill anyone and everyone they cross. Save the innocent. Submit to me."

The soldiers looked around nervously. Zeren pushed his way into the throne room. Copernicus' eyes locked on him. "Bow! Show them!"

Zeren looked pointedly at Redge. He shook his head.

"It's a lie! He has no other forces waiting."

Copernicus' head whipped around to Redge, his eyes bulging in shock and rage. His massive fist hit Redge in the chest, the force of it breaking his ribs, knocking him backward. The blow shook his heart off rhythm. Rahaxeris crashed on the floor next to him. Copernicus pulled his sword and raised it over Redge.

"Journey!" he tried to call out, but he didn't have the breath to manage any volume.

Copernicus jumped in alarm as the barrier was pounded and surrounded by slaves, all crazed to get at him. Their hands beat at the force field, but it held them back. He stared at them in disbelief for a second, then he laughed.

"You can't touch me! I am part wizard. No one can break through my power."

"I can." Rahaxeris stood, throwing the cuff around his neck to the ground. He lifted one finger to the barrier and traced a line down it. The blue force fractured like ice cracking.

"No!" Copernicus yelled. "Father, please!"

Rahaxeris flicked the fracture with his finger. The power fell into shards. Rahaxeris turned on Copernicus, and the crowd rushed forward, but he was gone. A portal closed where he had been standing.

A cry of despair rose up through the slaves. "He got away! We're still slaves! We'll never be free!"

Rahaxeris reached down and helped Redge to his feet. His skin blanched, and he nearly blacked out as his heart spluttered, off kilter. His knees gave out. Rahaxeris lowered him down again. He looked up into Journey's face, his head on her lap.

"I'm sorry," Redge said weakly. "I failed."

Rahaxeris knelt down beside him. "You didn't fail at all. He's lost his army. Your woman can keep them under control while we hunt him down. He's alone and on the run. All of his plans are ruined."

"Then he's more dangerous than ever, because he's desperate," Redge said.

Chapter Nineteen

Copernicus' portal was set to take him back to his ship, but instead of landing on the deck, he landed underwater. Water filled his lungs as he yelped in shock. He looked up to the surface of the water over his head, and then he looked down. The ship lay on the bottom just a few feet under his feet. *Forest*, he thought desperately. He pulled himself down and swam through the door on the deck's floor, searching for her body. Her cell was empty. He saw the holes in the ship's hull. His ability to stay under was running out. He stroked out of the sunken ship to the surface.

When his head broke through, he filled his lungs and exhaled in a guttural roar. He swam toward the closest shore; it would take hours to get there. He could just open another portal, but to where? He needed time to think. There was such sorrow inside him. He pushed it down and allowed wrath to take over. He had to if he was to survive. Had Shreve betrayed him? His diseased and twisted heart broke at the thought. Surely not. Shreve was his family. Someone else had taken Forest and killed Shreve before destroying his ship.

His fury escalated as his mind settled on Syrus. He'd never felt hate to this level before, and hate was something he was very experienced in. Syrus had found Forest because of his connection to her; it must be that. He should have killed Syrus in the very beginning. He realized that now.

The water slid over him as a new plan began to form in his mind. And he wouldn't sit around and wait, calculating the odds of success. He hadn't done that when he ran free through Regia before. Before he was sent to the wizards. His name was a legend because of that time, but this generation didn't know him or what he was capable of. If they thought he was ruthless, they had yet to know the half of it. Regia would cower and beg his forgiveness from a pool of blood. No more control.

But first things first… Forest. He opened a portal, knowing now where he wanted to go.

****

Rahaxeris personally saw to healing Redge. His entire ribcage was shattered and would cripple him if left to heal on its own, and Rahaxeris doubted anyone else was capable of making sure not one bone sliver was left loose. It only took one to travel through his veins and to his heart to kill him.

Rahaxeris made sure he was deeply unconscious before moving him from the throne room floor and back to his room. Journey sat beside him and held his limp hand while Rahaxeris worked. She didn't distract him by speed talking or falling into hysterical tears. She just held still and hummed quietly. Her voice nagged at the edge of his brain lightly.

"What are you doing?" Rahaxeris asked her.

"I'm giving him a good dream. Is my voice affecting you? I didn't think it would, but I can stop."

"Go ahead. I can shut it out. It won't mess with my concentration. I'm almost done anyway."

He ran his long, sharp fingers along Redge's torso, tracing where his ribs should be. His skin glowed red as his bones came back together. Rahaxeris repeated this simple action five times and was satisfied.

"I've got to go now," he said to Journey. "I have to stop Copernicus before things get worse."

"Worse?!"

"Oh, yes, my dear. Much worse. It's my sin that brought all of this about. It's my job to end it."

He struck the air with the flat of his hand. A portal opened for him. He looked back at Journey.

172

"Stick around, Storyteller. We need you." Then he was gone.

Rahaxeris landed in the main room of the *Rune-dy* headquarters. The smell was horrific. He held perfectly still in his shock as he looked down at the bodies on the floor. The blood was dry, the bodies bloated. They had been there for a few days. He couldn't deal with his feelings about it at the moment. He stepped carefully over his fellow priests, noting Menjel was not among them. He began searching the place.

"Menjel? Are you here?" he called.

Then he found him. Rahaxeris leaned down, looking closely at his body. His throat had been crushed and his skin was burned all over in snaking, lightning-like patterns. He didn't have to stain his brain to know who had done this. He and Syrus had a bit to discuss. But that would have to wait.

Rahaxeris closed himself away from the sights and smells in his private chambers. He wasn't wasting time. If anything, he was saving time. Clearing his mind of everything else, Rahaxeris focused all of himself on Copernicus. Where would he go? What would he do next? What was he feeling?

From everything Redge had told him and what he had seen and heard, Shreve was gone, or dead. Copernicus thought Forest was still his captive. He would want to cling to her. He had no one left. What would he do when he found her gone? She wasn't safe.

Rahaxeris opened another portal. He had to get to Copernicus before he found Forest again.

Rahaxeris landed in the water. He turned in a circle. No ship was in sight. He dove under the surface and looked down, spotting it on the bottom. He panicked for one second before he reminded himself that Redge told him Syrus had Forest. She wasn't down there.

****

Copernicus used his elf blood to go invisible as he approached the boundary of Forest's land. He could feel her. She was here. Why hadn't Syrus hidden her? Why keep her here? Then he felt the power in the air. He reached out and touched the blood lock. Ah, yes. Very nice work. But not good enough to keep him out. It was the first time he was thankful for what the wizards had done to him.

Chapter Twenty

The shattering sound was deafening. Forest covered her ears with her hands. Syrus grabbed up her glass sword and looked at her, lightning flashing in his eyes.

"Stay here."

"Syrus!" she called after him, but he was already outside.

Her heart constricted. She closed her eyes tight and held her breath, listening.

"Forest," Copernicus' disembodied voice whispered next to her ear.

"Show yourself," she said quietly.

He materialized next to the bed, soaked, dripping water, and a knife in his hand. Tears ran down her cheeks, and she reached out to him. "I missed you so much," she said.

He picked her up and held her against his chest. His heart beat so hard it drummed forcefully against her ribs. She could feel the blade flat against her back.

"I've been waiting for you, brother."

"You're actually happy to see me?" he asked.

"Of course I am. I love you."

His wild eyes filled with tears as he smiled, and shivers moved over his skin. "So long, I've thought about hearing you say that to me. I have to take you away from here, Forest."

"I know."

"I have to kill Syrus first. His hold on you must be broken."

"I know," she said again.

"Think you'll have better luck this time?" Syrus growled from the doorway.

Copernicus looked at him, tightening his grip on Forest. "Yes. I think I will... You're too afraid of what I might do to her. What are you prepared to offer me for her life?"

He turned Forest around in his arms like a shield over his chest, so she faced Syrus. The knife in his hand now pointed at her stomach. Syrus' eyes flashed, but the rest of his face remained blank.

"No, please, brother," she cried. "Don't hurt the baby. They need *you* to be their father."

Copernicus laughed mockingly at Syrus. "Did you hear her? She's betrayed you. She's mine now, because she *wants* to be. You have nothing. Perhaps you should just kill yourself and save me the trouble."

Syrus looked at the knife still pointing at Forest and raised one eyebrow. "Stop bluffing. You're not going to hurt her. You want her too much. And since I've obviously lost her, she's worthless to you as something to bargain with. You should stop holding her out like that because I've half a mind to kill the two-faced bitch myself."

Copernicus' eyes rounded as Syrus took a step forward. He set Forest on the floor and stood protectively in front of her. He dropped his knife and drew his sword. The metal sparked against the black glass as the two men crashed together in the middle of the small room.

They both were so tall, their weapons so big, and the space so confined, their strikes lost almost all effectiveness. The blades slid together as they both pushed against the other. Forest grabbed the knife off the floor next to her and crawled forward, slashing Copernicus across his Achilles heel. Blood sprayed over her face as he screamed in pain and stumbled sideways toward her.

176

He regained his balance, looking down at her, his sword lifted over her. The sound of something sailing through the air moved past his ear. Forest caught her sword. Syrus pushed him from behind as she reared up, stabbing the blade through Copernicus' chest.

Copernicus looked down, disbelieving, at the sword that ran him through. Blood trickled from the side of his mouth. He lifted his arm, still holding his sword. Forest turned the blade sideways, and using both hands, she pulled it upward through his chest to his chin, up the middle of his face until it broke out the top of his skull.

"That's for my baby!" Forest said to his split body on the floor.

Her arms fell, all the adrenaline gone. Syrus caught her as she went down. "Nice performance. Not that it wasn't painful to hear you say those things."

"Two-faced bitch?" she threw back at him.

He smirked as he carried her out of the room. He looked back at the body and grimaced. "I have to admit I'm a little surprised at your choice there. Rather gory for your taste, isn't it?"

"He threatened my baby. I could do worse."

He raised one eyebrow at her. "I believe you."

Rahaxeris burst into the house.

"It's over," Syrus told him. "Copernicus is dead."

"Oh!" he exhaled. "Where?"

Syrus nodded at the bedroom. Rahaxeris walked over and looked in. He turned back to them, his eyebrows raised, and his eyes rounded.

"You'd never convince me that wasn't personal," Rahaxeris said.

"That was all Forest. I don't think I would have cut his head open like that."

She scowled at Syrus. "He deserved it."

Merick and Netriet looked in the front door.

"It's all right," Syrus told them. "It's over."

Netriet ran in and knelt down next to Forest, placing her hand on her stomach. "Are you okay? Is the baby okay?"

"Calm down," Forest assured her. "We're both fine."

"You're covered in blood," Netriet argued.

"Not mine. Really, I'm okay. Not even a scratch."

Rahaxeris reached over Netriet and touched Forest's face. She met her father's gaze. "I thought I'd never see you again." He said. "I was sure you were dead."

"I'm not that easy to kill. I'm my father's daughter."

He smiled indulgently and shook his head. "You're full of big talk, girl." He looked at Syrus. "You're alive, and so is your child, because of him."

She rested her head on Syrus' shoulder. "I know it. Many times over."

Rahaxeris sighed. "Now, I've got to take the body to Halussis. The people need to know he's gone for good."

"That shouldn't be in question," Forest said. "All the slaves are free now."

"I'm still going to take him there. The fear and mystery around him needs to die as well."

"Come back soon, Father."

He nodded and smiled. They heard him open a portal in the bedroom, and then he was gone with the body.

Chapter Twenty One

All of Regia rejoiced and grieved simultaneously. Many lives had been lost in the hit on the castle. Since Copernicus had first come to Regia, until the moment he died, there wasn't an individual who hadn't lost something or someone to his evil. Few were lucky enough to have their loved ones returned to them when their slave marks disappeared.

A terrible shame clouded over those who had been slaves. Most didn't want to talk about it at all. Guilt, merited or not, pushed the people into a new frame of mind. Regia had a change of heart in the aftermath. The races came together in ways they never had before. Fervent discussions and groups broke out all over in support of Regia's republic. Forest was held up as a visionary who deserved absolute support.

But no one in power, nor the few who knew about the wizards, had time to catch their breaths. Journey met with the world leaders in the high council chamber at Fortress the day after the strike.

"I wish I could offer you more hope," she said sadly. "All I can tell you for sure is they are coming soon. There may be some power that can stand up to them, but if there is, I do not know it…I am not an ambassador of Illumistice, I'm an outlaw. Even if the governors of my world would listen to me, they would never agree to interfere. We have no power against them or influence anyway. It is only by chance that my world is not on the list along with Regia."

"How long do we have?" Zeren asked.

"The wizards are going after their main enemies first. Regia was not at the top their list. You may have months…if you're lucky perhaps years, but the clock is ticking."

All eyes turned to Rahaxeris.

"What can we do?" Zeren asked him.

"I don't know, yet. I'm working on it…I need everyone's unwavering support. If I call on you, you must answer me. If I need your services, time, or whatever else, I must not be refused. I'm going back to Kyhael. The *Rune-dy* headquarters is the best place for me to work. You must not fear it the way you might have in the past. The place's only purpose now will be finding an answer to this problem."

"Do we tell the people?"

The vote came back a majority no. It was agreed to keep it classified, at least for the time being. Forest was not at the meeting, still too weak to go anywhere. She was capable of walking from one end of her house to the other, and that was all.

After the meeting, Redge took Journey to meet Forest for the first time.

****

Syrus touched Forest on the shoulder, waking her gently from her nap. She blinked up at him and rubbed her eyes.

"Redge and Journey are here."

"Oh, okay." She ran her fingers through her hair and sat up against the pillows he propped behind her. "I want to talk to Redge alone first."

"All right. Just don't wear yourself out."

"I'm fine. Stop worrying."

He grunted in the back of his throat. "Yeah. I'm right on top of that," he said sarcastically.

Syrus left, and Redge came in, shutting the door behind him. Their eyes locked. She understood everything she saw in his face. He opened his mouth to speak, but she cut him off.

"No." She shook her head forcefully. "Do not ask my forgiveness. You have it. You had it before you ever laid a hand to me...I know what it's like to be a slave. I suffered under that burden much longer than you did."

Redge looked shocked. He opened his mouth, but again, she cut him off.

"That's all I will tell you about that. Don't ask me for more."

He nodded and went down on his knees next to the bed and took her hand, his face pained. "I still have to say it, Forest...I'm sorry."

"Okay. You said it. Now let it be over."

"I'll try my best, but I know that day will haunt me the rest of my life."

A small smile curved one side of her mouth. "You've got bigger problems, I hear. Ex-girlfriend back in town?"

His eyes lit up at the mention of Journey, and he grinned. "I brought her to meet you. She's nervous."

"Nervous about meeting me?"

"Yeah. She's met Syrus before, and she thinks he's *intimidating*. So she figures you're just like him in that way."

She arched a brow at him. "Am I?"

Redge snorted. "You can be intimidating, but not like him. Especially not now. He's changed."

181

She shook her head. "He's still just Syrus, but I know what you mean. Pain alters people."

He smirked. "I'm not talking about pain. I mean that scary shit his eyes do now when he's mad."

"Yeah, I'll admit that is...*intimidating*." She patted the top of his hand. "So...will you come back to work?"

"You're offering me my job back?"

"I need you. Will you consider it?"

His face went completely serious. "Yes, I'll come back to work. Thank you."

Forest didn't like to see him this humbled. She was ready for him to go back to the Redge she knew. She pulled her hand away from his and stretched. "Well, let me meet this goddess so I can get back to my nap, otherwise, Syrus will gripe that I'm wearing myself out, and he'll get short tempered."

"Okay." Redge got to his feet and left the room.

She only had a second to be apprehensive before Journey walked in. Forest couldn't help but be impressed by her beauty. Her skin was a perfectly even deep caramel. Black hair hung down her back in braids, accentuated with small metal clasps and beads. She was tall, probably only an inch or two under Redge's height, with small breasts and full hips. But her eyes were otherworldly, the irises a deep shade of pink, and they shimmered like jewels. The contrast of her eyes against the deep hue of her skin was stunning. She projected a warm, peaceful aura, which put Forest totally at ease.

"Come closer," Forest said. "Sit down."

Journey sat on the chair in the corner, looking nervous.

"Why did you come to Regia?" Forest asked a little forcefully, deciding on an unorthodox approach to getting to know the woman.

"Which time?"

"This time."

"I came to warn the love of my life that he was in danger."

"That's all?"

Journey smiled shyly. "I did have a few other desires, *hopes*, I should say. But warning him was enough to push me into the action I've longed to take since I originally left...I...I know it is to you that I must appeal for a permanent status in Regia."

"Why do you want to stay? Because you fear the repercussions of your actions once you get home?"

"No. I don't like the idea of facing them, but I would. I want to stay with Redge. I want to be with him for the rest of my life...I will do all I can to help Regia, I promise."

Forest smiled. "Redge is my friend. I want him to be happy. Submit the paperwork to my office, and I'll make sure your status is achieved. Once I can get to my wretched office, that is."

Journey's face lit up. "Thank you."

Forest pointed her finger at her. "Status can be revoked. If you hurt him, I'll boot your ass off world as fast as you can bat those pretty eyes."

Journey smiled. "Understood."

A knock sounded from the door, and Syrus poked his head in. "I think it's time," he said.

"Okay fine." Forest sighed before she realized he wasn't talking to her. He was looking intently at Journey, who nodded solemnly. "What's going on?"

183

Journey stood up, and Redge came into the room and held her hand. The air grew heavy, and Forest was instantly alarmed. She sat up straighter as Syrus came over and sat on the bed next to her.

"I have something terrible to tell you. It's going to hurt, a lot. I put it off because I knew in your weakened physical state the truth would put you back in danger. But you're stronger, and I can't stand lying to you."

Forest's eyes were round with apprehension. She clasped her hands on his shoulders, terrified to hear whatever it was, but convicted that she must. "What?" Her breathing was already fast, her pulse hammering.

He pulled her close to his chest. "The Fair...everyone's dead."

"No!" Agony rose up her core and stretched through her whole body.

Syrus held her painfully tight, as if he could absorb her pain. Her sobs racked her. All the strain went to her stomach and twisted deep inside.

"Journey?" Syrus said.

Journey stepped forward and began to sing. Her hypnotic voice broke through Forest's cries, and she quieted, her mind drifting. She reached inside Forest and grabbed the threads she needed. She took some from Syrus, Redge, and also herself. The song wrapped around Forest's broken heart and touched it softly, soothing the sting, but unable to erase it. Forest went limp in Syrus' arms, and he laid her back down, her eyes fully dilated.

After a long time, Redge and Syrus left the room, but Journey stayed by Forest throughout the night, helping her through the pain, anesthetizing it, so she could rest again. Once she was in a deep sleep, Journey came out, utterly exhausted.

She crashed into Redge's arms and yawned.

"She'll be okay," Journey told Syrus. "I'm glad I was here to help, though. You were right. She suffered terribly. She still will, but the level will be less. I can come back again if she needs me."

"Thank you. I'm in your debt."

Journey smiled at Syrus and shook her head. "I've read so many hearts in my life I never thought I'd find one that surprised me again. I love her… She's unique."

Syrus nodded. "Yeah, she is. Destiny gave me a real gift with her."

"We'll be at the castle if you need anything," Redge said.

It was midday as Redge and Journey finally left them and returned to Halussis.

Chapter Twenty Two

After a week, Forest was strong enough to be on her feet for an hour at a time. She was desolate about the Fair and determined to build a monument to her friends at the blighted location. It was a good place, she thought, to commemorate not only those who'd died there but also everyone Copernicus had murdered.

Forest had a hard time sleeping simply because her nightmares were so horrific. But in spite of that, she was getting stronger every day. The baby was now big enough for her to feel its movements, her stomach rounding out. She didn't see why she needed a guard anymore—the blood lock was broken, but Merhl was still hanging around frequently. Everyone else, though not actually guarding her, seemed to show up all the time.

Syrus was still on edge, but his focus turned to her pregnancy. He fussed over her so much she was ready to throttle him. But when she'd think about telling him to leave her alone, she couldn't stand the idea of him actually listening to her and going away, even if he did just go to work for the day. There were still terrible twinges she suffered deep in her abdomen, and nothing but Syrus' touch could ease the pain. She'd see him go through moments of total goofy happiness when he touched her stomach, even if he did try to hide it.

Forest really didn't know how she felt about anything, let alone her child. She was still so raw. She hoped, in time, she could experience the rushes of delight Syrus did.

"I want to go see Shi today," she told him over breakfast. "I feel much better. Will you take me?"

He looked at her with narrowed eyes, scrutinizing her total appearance.

186

"Really. I feel better. I don't want to stay long. I just need to check on her. It's been bothering me ever since Netriet told me Shi didn't answer when she and Merick went there."

"All right. Eat first."

"You're so bossy. Aren't you worried I'm going to get really fat?"

"No, get as fat as you like."

She snorted. "I'll remember you said that."

After breakfast, Merhl opened a portal to the Wood for them. They landed only a short ways from the Heart. The portal remained open, waiting to bring them back home when they were ready. Syrus picked her up and ran her away from the painful pull of the Heart's energy, setting her down on the beach by the smaller falls. She looked at him pleadingly. He understood what she wanted without her having to say it.

"I'll be close, but I'll give you some privacy."

"You're so good to me. Thank you."

He shrugged as though it was nothing and walked off through the trees.

Forest closed her eyes. *Shi? Where are you?*

For a long moment there was no answer.

Shi, please.

Shi's voice whispered in her head, as though from a great distance. "Forest. I'm overjoyed to see you are alive…You're pregnant!"

"Why won't you come out? I want to see you."

"I can't right now. If I let go of Ler, I'm afraid death will come and take him. I'm not ready to say goodbye."

187

"Wait. What?" Forest asked. "You're with him? Like together, together?"

"Yes."

Forest laughed. "That's wonderful…I mean, it is, right?"

"Yes. It's wonderful."

"Is that why you didn't come out and talk to Netriet when she came here?"

"I barely heard her. And then when I was about to try to talk to her, she left." Shi's voice broke with emotion. "The things I heard in her head. I thought for sure you were dead."

"You weren't the only one."

"Forest, this is very tiring, like being torn in two. I don't think I can manage it much longer. I'm sorry."

"Wait. What do you see when you look inside me? What can you tell me about the baby?"

"There is a strong magic in the child, perhaps too strong… Perhaps not. Time will tell. She is and will be very beautiful."

"It's a girl?"

"Oh, I'm sorry. Did you want that to be a surprise?"

Forest smiled and shook her head. "I like knowing. But I won't tell Syrus. He can wait it out… Shi, we've got real problems. I need your help. *Regia* needs your help. We have to stop the wizards."

"I love you, daughter…" Her voice trailed away. "But, to tell you the truth…I'm frozen…I can't…"

"Shi? Shi?!"

Nothing but a light breeze answered. Forest waited a few minutes in silence. Nothing stirred.

"Syrus?" she called out for him.

He was beside her in a flash. "Are you okay?" he asked.

Forest wiped at the tears on her cheeks. "Take me home."

Syrus tried to rush her into the open portal so she wouldn't feel too much of the pain she always felt being so close to the Heart, but she tried to stand it, looking toward Shi's crystal tree. Shi's tree looked different than the other nineteen surrounding the flames. The others were clear, as always, but Shi's had gone opaque as if it had indeed frozen, or was filled with smoke. Forest wanted to go up to the tree, but she couldn't get that close. Syrus wrapped his arm around her waist and pulled her back.

He insisted she lay down for a while when they got home. She didn't argue.

"What could that mean? The tree going all cloudy like that? I'm really worried. There's something wrong," Forest insisted.

Syrus smiled and kissed her. "Maybe nothing's wrong. You said they were back together. Maybe the smoke is from a fire they built."

"What?" Realization of what he was saying took a moment to sink in. "Ah, I guess. Like teenagers fogging the windows of a car."

"Now aren't you glad you weren't able to just walk right up and look inside?"

She snorted and snuggled down under the blanket he was pulling up over her. She looked up into his face as he smoothed the hair off her forehead.

"What is it?" he asked.

She opened her mouth then closed it and shook her head. "Nothing. I'm tired and just buying trouble."

He tapped his finger over his heart. "I feel you're worried about something."

"Worry is my constant state right now," she deflected.

"Yeah. Mine too."

Chapter Twenty Three

Journey opened her eyes in the dark, coming awake sharply as though startled. She sat up in bed next to Redge, pulling the thin cover around her bare skin. She looked down at him. He slept peacefully, his arm outstretched to her, lying in wait to snuggle her back into his side. She gasped as his steady pulse filled her ears like a base drum. A nameless fear began to peck at her heart like the beak of a predator bird. Sharp tiny bites over and over, taking pieces of her away and swallowing them. *What was wrong?*

She read his heart as he slept, searching for the origin of her dread. She knew his heart so well. She saw the alteration immediately, and it cut like a blade thrust down her throat. *No. Not this. Please, not this.* She shook herself and looked again. Her name was Kylie. Redge's destined life mate's name was Kylie. The knowledge of this stranger filled his heart, under the surface, where it would lay dormant until he saw her for the first time. It would be tomorrow. That was why it was manifesting in his heart. He would meet Kylie tomorrow, and his love for Journey would die as quickly as a candle flame blown out, and forgotten almost as quickly.

Redge woke to Journey pressing down on him. She was kissing him painfully hard. The tears falling from her eyes landed on his face. She pulled at him with total desperation. He tried to sit up, but she pushed him back.

"What's wrong?"

The moonlight through the window glistened on her flowing tears. She didn't answer.

"Journey, what's wrong?" he demanded.

"Don't talk. Just love me, right now. Break me down the way you did before…the way you did when you first got me back."

He grabbed her by the shoulders and used only as much force as he had to hold her back. "No. Absolutely not. I will not make love to you while you are crying and upset. Tell me what is wrong. I'm freaking out here."

"Please." She swiped at the tears on her cheeks. "I'll stop crying."

He moved away from her and got out of bed, wearing only a loose pair of lounge pants. She couldn't stop herself; she came after him. He handed her a robe. She slid her arms through it and belted it. Then she crashed into him again, wrapping her arms around his torso. He held on to her hesitantly, rubbing his hands up and down her back as if she were cold. Abruptly, he stopped, and his whole body went rigid.

"You're leaving me," he said. "Aren't you?"

"Yes. At dawn. I'm leaving while I can, and so I don't have to see…" She cried.

"Don't have to see what?" he yelled, pulling away from her.

The words lodged in her throat and choked her. "You…stop…loving…me."

"What? What are you talking about?"

"This is the end of us, Redge. These are the last hours we have before our love dies. Or, rather your love for me dies. I will go on loving you forever…I saw it there in your heart. Just now, while you slept. You'll meet your destined life mate tomorrow. Kylie. Forgive me, but I'm not going to stick around and watch while you forget me."

His mouth hung open. He looked like she'd just stabbed him in the heart. When he didn't say anything she became so angry her vison blurred.

"I wanted to leave with a sweet memory, but I can see that isn't going to be. Fine. I'm leaving now."

"Wait."

"For what? There's nothing. You want your mate. Of course you do. Who wouldn't? I get it. The bond is something I can never give you. I hope Regia survives…I hope you do. I know you'll be happy, and maybe one day I'll be noble enough to find some kind of selfless joy in knowing you're happy. But I doubt it. Both of you can burn in hell."

She bolted from the room.

"Journey!"

She ignored his call, running down the hall and through another door. The room was empty except for a single ogre. Perfect. She could grasp the golden current to take her home, but there was one thing left for her to do in Regia.

"Please." She walked up to the ogre. "Please open a portal for me to the Wolf's Wood."

He gave her a little bow and complied. The rushing took her away from the castle, away from Redge. When her bare feet hit soft sand, she fell on her hands and knees and cried out an involuntary sound of her heart ripping in two. She saw nothing really, just smudges and blurs of color, her eyes submerged under the deep ocean of her tears. She rolled over onto her back and looked up at the sky as the hateful dawn slapped her. She closed her burning eyes and took a deep shuddering breath, trying to calm the tremor in her chest.

She stood. It was terrible to linger. She would see what she came here to see, and then she would leave. Journey blinked at the silver purple waterfall, clearing her eyes. She didn't stare. She saw it, now she would see the Heart, and then she would leave.

Where are you going, Journey? His voice whispered in her head. *I love you. You. You're everything to me.*

Her heart stilled. He kept on. Whispering in short sentences, just as he had every day for all these past years.

Help me.

Stay with me.

Don't go.

Please.

There is no one else. There never will be.

She heard something behind her and turned around.

There he was, a piece of parchment burning in his hand. He dropped it as the flame turned it to ash.

"Why did you follow me?"

"Because I have no destiny. I reject anything and everything that says I cannot be with you."

"It doesn't work like that," she insisted.

"Yes it does… Everyone has a choice. Even those who have destined life mates. You can always reject it."

"Why would you? It has a legendary agony."

"Perhaps your gift has spared me that. And Kylie as well. No one knows who or when it will happen to them, and you told me. So, I've already rejected it. Before it ever happened. It hurt, I'll admit, but just for a moment. Or maybe the pain was terrible but I couldn't really feel it. It was nothing to the pain of watching you run from me. I will not live my life without you, Journey. I reject that."

The healer in her came out. "But you hurt her, too, didn't you? She didn't do anything to deserve that."

"Whoever she is, she's better off without me."

"But…"

"But what? You just said she could burn in hell."

"No, I said the both of you could burn in hell," she corrected.

"Well, it's done. And there's nothing you can do about it." He reached out and pulled her into his arms. She looked into his eyes as he cupped her cheek with his hand. "Stay with me. *You're* my destiny."

Her tears threatened to come back. "You really rejected her?"

"Read my heart."

She did. She pushed through the surface and plunged its depths, but she was the only woman there.

"Please, Journey. Say you'll stay with me."

She closed her eyes and took a deep breath. When she opened her eyes again, he was smirking at her.

"Don't act like you don't want to." His voice was tauntingly confident.

"Why are you so cocky?"

He quirked a brow at her, still smirking. "I'm your slave, remember? And you did just try to rape me few minutes ago."

"I did not!"

He caught her chin in his hand. "Did too."

Her cheeks heated, but she recovered quickly. "It's common knowledge that arrogance is often just a bluff to cover insecurities…I think I'll have to stay so as not to damage you permanently. Your ego is way too fragile to handle a blow like me leaving."

"Whatever." He threw back at her.

He silenced her giggle, kissing her until she couldn't breathe and her head spun.

"Why did you come here?"

She had to blink a few times and focus on his question. "Oh…I've never seen the Heart. I was determined to before I left."

"Well, let's go see it then."

She took his hand and let him lead her to the Heart.

Journey stared at the Heart for a long time, feeling it deep inside her. It wasn't just called the Heart, it *was* a heart. The truest heart she had ever encountered, and it was diseased. Regia's heart was confused, poisoned, and erratic. But it held a well of power she couldn't comprehend. Now she understood why the wizards wanted Regia. It was the Heart.

She came right up to the crystal trees and touched their cold trunks with her fingertips. She touched them all in turn, except for the one that was different, cloudy. Journey gazed into the trunk and saw the image of two people, entwined lovers, frozen and unmoving, like an etching inside the crystal.

Redge waited for her a few paces back. She walked back to him, disturbed and contemplating.

"There's something wrong here... And I think I can help fix it."

Chapter Twenty Four

The most important people in the world to Forest stood around her at the blighted site that had been the Fair. She'd cried herself out over the loss of her friends who had died there, and now her eyes were over-dry and achy. The twelve-foot spire of alabaster-like Belliss stone from Kyhael was already in the center of the area, ready to have the names of the dead carved into it.

She looked over at Merick and Netriet. "Are you ready?"

They both nodded.

"We don't want to forget anyone."

"We won't," Merick reassured her.

Rahaxeris stepped forward and placed his hand on the stone and looked back at Forest.

"Tek, Martia, Renee, Koll…" She listed their names as Rahaxeris moved his hand over the surface, carving the names with his power. Whenever she paused for even a second, Merick chimed in, listing off names she hadn't spoken yet. Soon every side was covered in names.

"That's all of them," Merick said heavily.

Rahaxeris stepped back, his job finished, giving Syrus space to come up and begin his part. Syrus laid both of his hands flat on the smooth stone and muttered a few words under his breath. A surge of red light went into the stone from his hands. The light pooled into the carved names, lighting them up red. He stepped back.

"You have a few minutes," Syrus said to Forest, Merick, and Netriet.

They came forward and touched each name in turn. Forest thought of the memory she wanted left behind for Tek as her index finger traced the carved letters of his name. Syrus' power grabbed at the memory she offered and held it fast in the stone. She pulled her hand back and moved to the next one. Merick offered the stone his memories and so did Netriet.

"Did it work?" Forest asked Kindel, who was witnessing and waiting.

Kindel stepped forward and touched one name at random. He'd never met the person named, but as he touched the carved letters, the face and voice came into his mind along with the pleasant memory Forest had left there.

"It worked," Kindel said quietly, effected deeply by the memorial. "It's beautiful."

Ena walked up to it and touched it. She took a longer time than Kindel, slowly absorbing the memories. When she came away, there were tears in her eyes.

"How do we protect it?" Merick asked.

"Merhl?" Forest looked over at the ogre.

He came forward, moving his hands around energy and power none of them could see. A ripple moved down from the top of the monument and rolled down to the ground. Merhl stepped back.

"Anyone will be able to touch the stone and receive the memories left behind, but no one will be able to deface the stone or break it. It is safe."

Forest hugged him tightly. "Thank you, Merhl."

His massive arms swallowed her up. "It was no problem…Oh, here, before I forget." He held out his hand, a new End of the Bridge in his palm, set into a ring. "I heard you lost your other one in your ordeal."

She smiled and took it. "Sometimes I don't know what I'd do without you."

Merhl blushed and shook his head.

The afternoon grew cold, a mist stretched over the ground. Everyone left the memorial, dropping off one by one, until no one was left but Forest, Syrus, and Rahaxeris. Syrus rubbed Forest's shoulders in an attempt to warm her against the chill in the air.

Rahaxeris faced her and touched her distended stomach gently. "Not much longer. I have to leave Regia for a while, but I'll be back before the baby comes. I promise."

"Okay, Father. Be careful."

He nodded and left them alone.

Syrus kissed the top of her head and looked over at the monument. "It's beautiful, Forest. You did a good job."

"I didn't do much. You and Dad and Merhl did most—"

"It was your idea." He pulled her tightly against his side. "Let's go home."

Epilogue

Two months later...

The *Rune-dy* headquarters were a mess. Rahaxeris was working tirelessly to find a solution to protect Regia from the wizards. But there in Kyhael, he was a one-man show. Sure, there were others kicking ideas around and having as much or less success as he was. He'd started world jumping out of desperation, trying to call on the benevolence or resources of other places for help or answers.

Not everyone had turned a cold shoulder, but he was also pressed for time to get back before Forest gave birth. She went into labor in the middle of the night, in a terrible storm. The summons arrived for him to come quickly.

It was unconventional for the father of a woman to oversee the birth, but then everything with Forest seemed to be unconventional. She'd asked him to deliver the baby because of her constant fear that something was amiss. So he'd agreed.

Syrus waited it out, outside in the storm. It was customary for Regian fathers to not witness the birth of their children. So he banished himself to the garden despite the fact it was pouring rain. Even through the thunder crashing over his head, Syrus heard his child cry out for the first time.

A few moments later, Rahaxeris came out. "It's a girl. Forest has named her Tesla."

"Tesla?"

"She said that's the name she chose because she's the daughter of lightning."

Syrus' smile lit up the night, and he made to go inside to meet his daughter. Rahaxeris grabbed him roughly by the arm and stopped him.

"Wait. This isn't the joyous occasion you think it is. You need to be prepared before you go in there."

"What?" Syrus demanded.

"There's something very wrong with the baby."

The End

A note from Tenaya

Hello Dear Reader! Thank you for coming back to Regia with me!
It is my fondest hope that you enjoyed it, and that you will come
back again in the spring for the next book, Blood Lock. The final
two books are the closest to my heart and I cannot wait to share the
conclusion of The Legends of Regia with you. Be sure to sign up
for my newsletter, on tenayajayne.com, so you never miss
important news, giveaways, and release dates.

Thank you so much for your continued support! I cannot tell you how
much it means to me.

Love,

Tenaya

www.ingramcontent.com/pod-product-compliance
Lightning Source LLC
Chambersburg PA
CBHW032000170626
46807CB00006B/2581